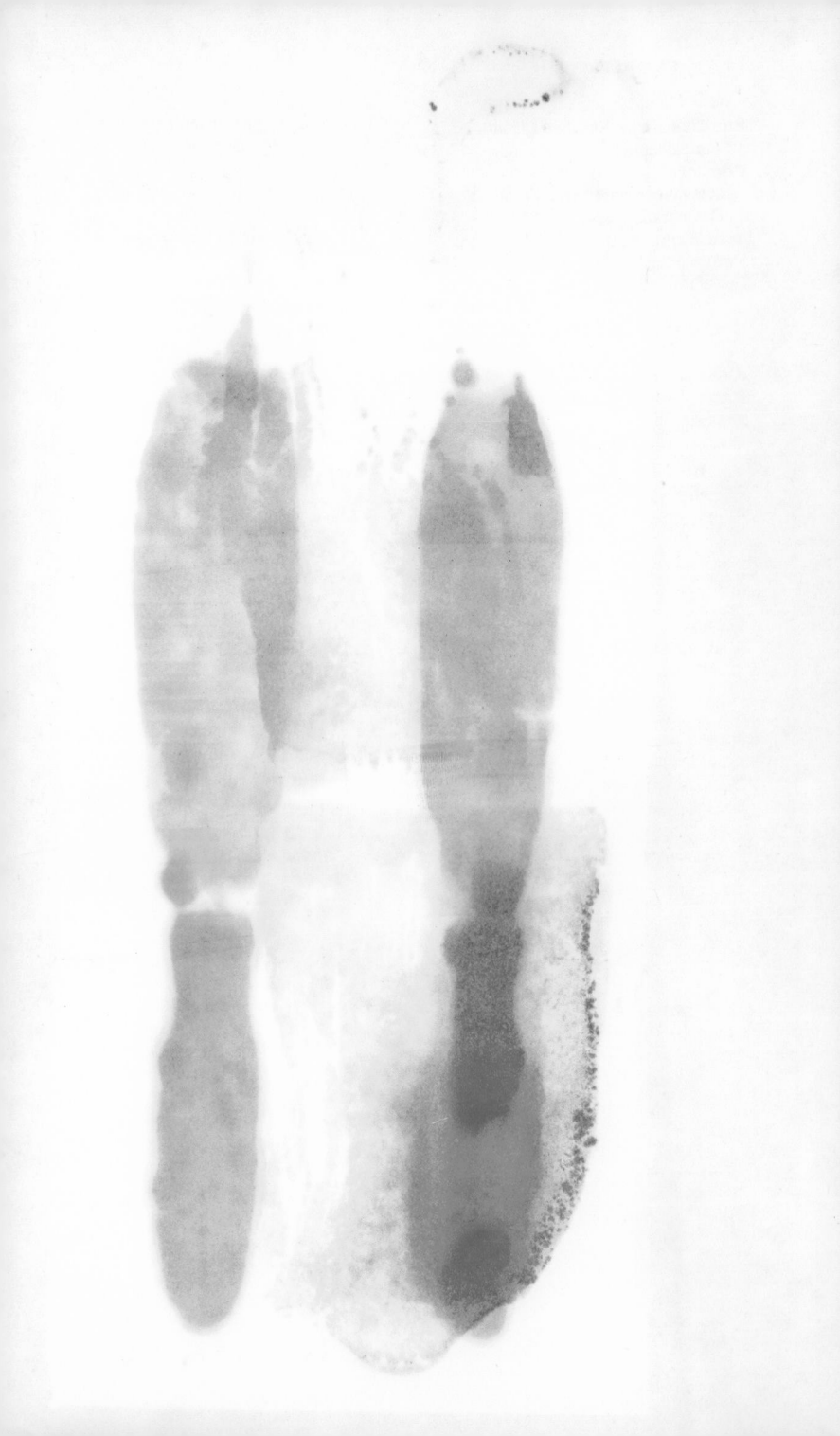

CREATIVE WOMAN MYSTERIES®

What a Picture's Worth

Susan Page Davis

Annie's®
AnniesFiction.com

Library of Congress-in-Publication Data
What a Picture's Worth / by Susan Page Davis
p. cm.
I. Title
2013900607

AnniesFiction.com
(800) 282-6643
Creative Woman Mysteries®
Series Editor: Shari Lohner

10 11 12 13 14 | Printed in China | 9 8 7 6 5 4 3

— 1 —

Shannon McClain checked the lock on the front door of her craft store and gazed out over the "Closed" sign. On the street outside, people heading home for the night surged along the sidewalk. In half an hour, Apple Grove's busiest street would be calm and nearly deserted. That suited Shannon just fine—she loved the slow pace of small-town life.

"Want me to lock up?" Essie Engleman, the store manager, called from across the room as she unplugged the vacuum cleaner.

"I'll do it. You go on home." Shannon walked over to the checkout area and picked up the zippered money bag she'd left on the counter a moment earlier. "I came out even to the penny tonight."

"Great."

"I'd better put this in the safe while you're still here." Shannon walked with her down the short hallway at the back of the store.

Essie wheeled the vacuum into the storage room, and Shannon entered her office. She unlocked the file drawer where they kept their handbags during the day and then turned her attention to the safe. She quickly unlocked it, placed the bank bag inside, and shut the door.

Essie breezed in and took her purse from the open drawer. "Good night!"

"See you in the morning." Shannon picked up her purse and glanced around her office to be sure she wasn't forgetting anything. Satisfied she had everything she needed, she returned to the main part of the store and switched off the lights.

The faint glow of light spilling down from the artists' lofts on the second floor made her pause. As far as she knew, none of the artists were still working in their lofts. The last one to leave, Fredo Benson, a rather eccentric painter, had gone home around four o'clock.

She sighed and headed up the stairs. Reaching the top, she saw that the light came from Fredo's loft, and his door stood slightly ajar. Puzzled, she walked over and knocked on it.

"Fredo? Are you in there?"

Silence greeted her. She nudged the door open a few more inches and peeked in. The room appeared to be empty. Only Fredo's mounted paintings stared back at her.

It was a small room, about ten by ten feet, and the upper level at the Paisley Craft Market & Artist Lofts held twelve of them. Renting the rooms to local artists brought Shannon extra profits and drew in customers who were interested in a variety of crafts and fine arts. Some of the artists even offered classes in their lofts or in the coffee shop downstairs.

Apparently, Fredo had forgotten to lock his door when he left. He'd also neglected to turn off a lamp on his worktable, which was cluttered with brushes, tubes of paint, drawing pencils, and paint-smeared rags. In fact, Fredo's entire space looked quite untidy, especially considering he'd only occupied the loft for a few weeks. But he'd started out with a bang, offering classes in oils and acrylics, and students streamed in and out several days a week to study with him. Shannon wasn't sure yet what to make of the flamboyant man who had sliced off the bottom part of his left ear in homage to his idol, Vincent van Gogh, but overall, he seemed to be a good addition to the roster of artists in residence.

She stepped inside and reached out to push the switch on the lamp, but a painting on an easel caught her eye, and she froze. With her hand in midair, she stared at the eerily familiar landscape.

My garden.

Had Fredo Benson ever been inside the Paisley mansion? If not, how could he possibly produce such a detailed picture of the private garden in the back, an area not visible from the driveway?

She pulled in a deep breath and willed her pulse to slow down. *No need to panic—is there?* It was a very nice painting. In fact, if the question of Fredo's access to the garden hadn't been bothering her, she might have considered buying it to hang in her office. She would be sure to ask him how he knew so much about her home in the morning.

Glancing at the table a second time, Shannon's gaze fell on something else—a sketchbook, lying between a tube of yellow ochre paint and a pad of palette paper.

I really shouldn't go snooping through his things ...

But she hesitated only a fraction of a second before flipping open the cover.

The sight of the sketch on the first page overruled any guilt she'd felt about spying. The drawing showed a fern-lined pathway with a lake in the distance—*her* lake, behind the Paisley mansion.

Her pulse pounded as she turned the page to the next picture. It was a very good likeness of Old Blue, her 1955 Ford truck—the pickup she'd inherited from her late grandmother, Victoria Paisley, along with the mansion and the craft market. The old thing was a bucket of bolts, but she'd come to love it since she'd moved to Apple Grove. It appeared that Fredo also liked the truck, but what kept her adrenaline flowing was the fact that he'd sketched it parked *inside* her garage. She recognized all the tools and folded patio chairs that hung on the walls.

My garage.

Stunned, she leafed through the pages of the sketchbook and found four more sketches, all of which portrayed different views of the grounds around the mansion. The sketch that bothered her most, however, mocked her from the last page Fredo had used in the sketchbook. It held a highly detailed drawing of the black marble equestrian statue that stood in her foyer, near the main staircase. The giant horse reared on its hind hooves, and below it lay a snake, coiled and ready to strike. The two-story-tall piece had come with the house, and she loved it. The figure was so lifelike that Shannon could almost hear the stallion scream.

In her mind, she pictured every detail of the foyer, including the heavy front door and the frosted sidelights that flanked it; she felt certain no one could possibly gather that much detail about the statue by simply peeking in a window.

A wave of unease ran through her. There was only one way the moody artist could've drawn the pictures with such accuracy.

Fredo Benson had been inside her house.

Shannon scooped up the sketchbook and hugged it to her body. Her gaze darted around the loft space, searching for anything else that might betray him.

She considered taking the painting as well but decided against that. It was too large and cumbersome to carry easily. But she *was* taking the sketchbook, and she would definitely ask him about it first thing in the morning.

Trying to squelch her anxiety, Shannon turned off the light and locked the door. As she descended the stairs, she mulled over what she'd just discovered. She wouldn't tell her twins, Alec and Lara, about it. The whole thing was too creepy, and she didn't want them to worry. The kids had only been in the States for a few months, and already they'd endured one very stressful—and dangerous—murder investigation. They planned to stay with her in Apple Grove until the fall semester started at Portland State University. That day was fast approaching. It would be better if they left for school in a few weeks *not* worrying about her.

When she got home, Deborah, the live-in housekeeper, had supper waiting.

"Mum's home, c'mon Alec!" Lara called cheerfully as she met Shannon in the front hall. "Wait until you taste the lasagna—it's fabulous! I helped Deborah make it."

"It smells wonderful." Shannon gave her a quick hug. "I'm starved."

"Hi, Mum." Alec jogged down the stairs, his eyes riveted on the dining room. "I'm starving too. Can we eat now?"

Shannon chuckled. "I wouldn't dare try and stop you."

They all gathered around the table and began to eat— Deborah included. Not long after Shannon had inherited the mansion, she realized that Deborah had been much more than a housekeeper and cook to her late grandmother. She'd been a dear and trusted friend, someone who had shared her meals with Victoria at the family table. Shannon saw no reason to change that practice.

As Shannon enjoyed the delicious meal, she tried to focus on the lively chatter around her, but she couldn't keep her mind from wandering to the painting and the sketches.

"Hey, Mum." Alec's voice pulled her from her thoughts. "Can I take those old pistols out of the case in the hallway?"

Shannon knew he referred to the pair of antique cap-and-ball dueling pistols mounted in a glass case on the wall. "Let's leave them alone until I can get an antique firearms expert to look at them. They're probably not loaded, but you never know."

"Fine." Alec sighed. "It's not like I don't have enough to do, getting ready for university."

Lara moaned. "Oh, did you have to mention it?"

"I thought you were eager to start school in Portland," Alec said. "What's wrong, are you afraid you won't be able to survive without your boyfriend, Chaz?" He batted his eyelashes and flashed a goofy grin.

Lara glared at him. "Not that it's any of *your* business, but we've decided just to be friends. I'm not ready for a serious relationship right now."

Shannon's heart leapt with joy at the news, but she was careful to keep her expression neutral.

Lara continued, "I'm sad because it's been so much fun here with Mum and Deborah, I sort of don't want to leave."

Shannon smiled. "Well, this is our home now, so you'll be coming back here often. I'm sure you'll be able to visit on weekends."

"It's going to take a while for this place to feel like home to me." Alec looked around the elegant dining room as he spoke, his gaze lingering on the silver sconces, the inlaid side tables, and the crystals on the chandelier. "Sometimes I feel like we're living in a museum now."

"I can understand that," Shannon said. "I had similar thoughts when I first moved in. I may decide to cozy it up a bit in the future, but right now, I'm too busy at the craft market—and besides, I rather like feeling that this was exactly the way my grandmother liked it."

Lara nodded, looking up at the chandelier and crown molding. "It's fun thinking about how she must have loved this house, and how she collected each piece of the decorations. It looks like she put a lot of thought into it."

"Oh, she did," Deborah interjected. "She absolutely loved art and antiques. After she was widowed, those became her passions. Every item you see in this house had special meaning for her. If she decided she didn't like a piece for some reason, she immediately got rid of it."

"Maybe we should do the same," Alec said with a chuckle.

"Oh, hush you." Shannon scowled at him. "What's there to dislike?"

"The sculptures." He reached for a second helping of lasagna. "They're a bit odd, don't you think?"

"I'm not crazy about the big horse in the foyer." Lara shuddered in her typical dramatic fashion. "But I find most of the pieces to be quite lovely."

Shannon was happy to have the conversation steered to the treasures she'd inherited, and she managed to push her worries about Fredo to the back of her mind for the remainder of the meal. But later that evening, as they all separated for the night, she couldn't help herself—she *had* to issue a safety reminder to the kids. It would be foolhardy not to, in light of what she'd found in Fredo's loft.

"Kids, don't forget, while I'm at the store tomorrow ..." she began, and the twins turned to look at her expectantly. "No, make that *anytime* I'm not here, please make sure the alarm is set and the doors are locked—especially if you leave the house."

The twins exchanged exasperated looks.

"Of course. We wouldn't want those dueling pistols to be heisted." Alec's smile softened his words.

"Really, Mum, you worry too much." Lara shook her head, her dark red hair rippling.

Alec headed for the staircase. "I'll bet Grandma Paisley didn't fret so much."

Lara scowled at his back. "Shows how much you know. If she never worried, she wouldn't have this high-powered security system, now would she?" She turned to face Shannon. "But I wish we didn't need it. I couldn't remember the code yesterday, and I was afraid it would ring in at the police station before I could turn it off."

Shannon nodded. "It is a bother, I know, but I think it's necessary. Besides, my grandmother didn't have a security system. I installed it after I arrived—once I'd had the pleasure of meeting our less-than-welcoming kin."

"Oh, right." Alec looked back, his expression morphing

into concern. "I sort of forgot about what you went through before we got here. Sorry."

"Apology accepted," Shannon said. "And thank you *both* for humoring your Mum by agreeing to keep the house locked up tight at all times while I'm gone."

The brief look of renewed annoyance that passed between the twins did not escape Shannon's notice.

"Sure. Night, Mum," Lara called as she followed Alec up the stairs. "See you at breakfast."

"Good night."

Shannon surveyed the foyer, remembering her very first glimpse of the room—the marble table, the statuary, the wall niches for art, and the imposing plasterwork on the ceiling. She loved this room. In fact, she loved the whole house. Although she'd never known her grandmother, she felt that she now knew a lot about her through the things Victoria had loved.

Did Victoria know Fredo? Did she invite him here so he could sketch some of the graceful views and the statue in the foyer? It didn't seem likely. When Fredo had come to the craft market less than a month earlier to ask about renting one of the artists' lofts, he'd presented himself as a stranger would. Surely if he'd known her grandmother personally, he would have commented on—or at least offered his condolences about—Victoria's passing. Shannon frowned as she slowly climbed the stairs. It was too odd by half.

— 2 —

The blare of the phone beside her bed jerked Shannon from sleep. Instinctively, she rolled and grabbed for the receiver—anything to stop the noise!

"Hello?" She blinked at the digital clock. *One in the morning—who would call at this unearthly hour?*

"Mrs. McClain?" said a man's voice.

Shannon's pulse doubled. "Speaking. Who is this?"

The man identified himself as an employee of the security company that monitored her home and business. "The alarm was tripped at Paisley Craft Market," he said. "Would you like me to call the police?"

"Absolutely! I'm heading down there now." Shannon slammed the phone down without waiting for a reply. She threw on jeans, a cotton pullover shirt, and a pair of clogs. Grabbing her purse and cellphone, she dashed out of her room.

She nearly collided with Deborah, who stood wrapped in her blue chenille bathrobe at the top of the steps, her short white hair askew.

Deborah stifled a scream and gripped the banister for balance, her eyes wide. "I heard the phone ring. Is everything all right?"

"Sorry I scared you." Shannon patted the older woman on the arm. "Yes. The alarm went off at the store. I'm heading there now." She hurried past her and down the stairs.

Deborah followed close behind. "Want me to go with you?"

"No, I—"

"Mum?" At the sound of Alec's voice, they both looked up. He stood on the landing in his boxers and a gray T-shirt, stifling a yawn. "What's going on?"

"I'm going to the craft store. The alarm was tripped."

"I'll go with you." He seemed suddenly awake. "Won't take me but a second to throw on some clothes."

Before Shannon could protest, Alec turned and scooted for his room. She wished he hadn't woken up. Now she had to wait for him, or he'd worry. He reappeared less than a minute later, wearing jeans and running shoes and pulling on a long-sleeved shirt as he bounced down the stairs.

"Want me to drive?" he asked, always eager to put his temporary international driver's license to use. Getting his license was one of the first things he'd done when he arrived from Scotland. Lara had one too, but she didn't use it as often as her brother did. She disliked driving the "antique lorry," as she derisively referred to Shannon's truck.

"Sure." Shannon handed him the keys and glanced at Deborah.

"Don't worry about a thing here." Her housekeeper waved them toward the door. "I'll explain everything to Lara if she wakes up."

"Thanks."

Alec punched in the security code that would allow them to leave without setting off the alarm.

"And I'll reset that," Deborah added, striding toward them. "Go on."

"Thank you."

Shannon followed Alec's quick strides to the garage. They climbed into the truck, and the 1955 Ford's engine leaped to life under his touch.

Boys, she thought. Although she and the truck had made friends, they'd gotten off to a rocky start. But it seemed to her that the temperamental old pickup would do anything for Alec.

Without so much as a choke or gasp from Old Blue, Alec steered it out of the driveway and onto the main road. "So, what exactly happened?"

"The alarm was tripped. Why? I'm not sure." Shannon ran a nervous hand through her unruly red curls. "It's probably nothing. Maybe a mouse set off a motion detector or something. But the security company did call the police."

"Good."

Ten minutes later, they arrived at the store. A police SUV sat parked before the door, and as Shannon climbed down from the truck, a uniformed officer met her on the sidewalk.

"Evening, ma'am," the policeman said. "Are you the owner?"

"Yes, I'm Shannon McClain, and this is my son, Alec."

"I'm Officer Doan. Officer Brownley's around back. It appears the back door has been forced."

Shannon gasped. "Someone actually broke in?"

"Yes, they jimmied the door. If you'd like to come around with me, I'll show you. We took a quick look inside, and we don't think anyone's in the building now, but we'll do a thorough search before we leave, to be sure. Chief Grayson's on his way here too."

They rounded the building to find Officer Brownley examining the doorframe with his flashlight. "Hello, Mrs. McClain." He gave a sober nod to Shannon and Alec. "It would be best if you both wait out here while we complete our sweep of the building. After we're sure the burglar's not inside, we'll escort you in, and you can look around and tell us if anything's been taken."

"That sounds like a good plan." Shannon examined the splintered doorframe in the dim light, dismayed by the damage she saw.

Both officers entered the building, and she and Alec waited outside. A breeze ruffled the leaves. Shannon found herself shivering as she peered into the darkness behind the building, where the glow of streetlights didn't penetrate.

"You OK, Mum?"

Shannon rubbed her arms and nodded. "I wish I'd grabbed a sweater before I ran out the door."

He stepped close and put an arm around her. "I'll keep you warm."

"Thanks." Once again she was struck by Alec's maturity— and height. He was as tall now as his father, John, had been. He had John's rugged build too. She cuddled gratefully into the curve of his arm. "I hope they don't take long in there."

"Me too," Alec said. "This is kind of strange, don't you think? I mean, robbing a craft store? It's not like one would expect a big payout for the trouble, like it's a bank."

"True."

Officer Brownley appeared in the doorway. "All clear, ma'am. You can step inside now. Sorry to keep you waiting."

"Better safe than sorry." Shannon ducked into the back hallway and peered into her office. "Och, they've definitely been through my desk."

Papers and office supplies were scattered across the desk. One of its drawers hung partway open, and a couple of pens and a paperclip lay on the rug below.

"All right, don't touch anything," Officer Brownley said. "What else looks out of place?"

Shannon turned slowly, observing the room. The file cabinets and shelves of supplies looked untouched, but she wasn't sure she'd know unless the intruder had made a mess of them, as he had the desk. Her worktable appeared to be as she'd left it—bare, except for several bead containers.

As she completed the turn, her breath caught. "The safe's been moved."

"Where was it before?" Officer Brownley asked.

"Flush with the wall." The heavy safe had been pushed about a foot from its usual spot, toward the door.

"My guess is the thief tried to take it, but it was too heavy." Officer Brownley scrawled a note on his pad. "At least it doesn't appear to be damaged. Why don't you walk through the rest of the store with me and see if you notice anything else that's not right."

She opened the door to the storage room across the hall and switched on the light. "As far as I can tell, this room hasn't been disturbed."

"Likely they didn't come in here." The officer accompanied her to the main part of the store, and Alec followed silently behind them.

Shannon's gaze swept over the counters and displays.

"We've looked behind and under all the fixtures," Officer Brownley said. "We couldn't see that anything was broken."

"Thanks." She strode to the arched doorway that connected the main sales area to the coffee shop, where artists held classes and charity groups met to work on projects. "Nothing amiss in here."

"Chief Grayson's here," Officer Doan called out from behind the checkout counter.

Shannon hurried to greet Grayson. "Chief, thanks for coming."

"No problem." The chief gave Alec a clipped nod. "Hello."

"Hello, Chief," Alec said. "Nice wake-up call, huh?"

"I'm used to it—happens fairly often at my house." Grayson shifted his focus to Shannon. "The alarm company called us to report the break-in, and Officer Doan tells me your office seems to have been the main target. Is this correct?"

"That's right. So far I haven't noticed anything missing, but I haven't gone through my desk thoroughly. We think the burglar tried to take the safe. Did Officer Doan tell you?"

Grayson nodded. "What's in it?"

"Not much." Shannon tucked a strand of hair behind her ear. "I take the receipts to the bank daily. There was less than two hundred dollars left when I cashed out tonight."

"The register's empty?" Grayson asked.

"Yes. I never leave any money in it overnight."

"Did you leave the drawer open?"

Shannon gave him a confused look. "No."

"Some owners leave the empty drawer open so it's obvious there's no money in the register. Keeps potential thieves from messing with it. You might want to do that in the future." Grayson looked at his officers. "Was the register opened?"

"Don't think so," Officer Brownley said. "It's shut now, and there's no sign that it was tampered with."

"Good. Shannon, would you open it to make sure the burglar didn't do anything to it? And maybe you want to check the contents of the safe too—make sure nothing is missing."

"Certainly." Shannon pulled her keys from her purse, unlocked the cash register, and opened the drawer. As she'd expected, it was empty except for a couple of coupons in one of the slots they used for special items like traveler's checks.

Grayson leaned in and eyed it, then nodded. "Let's have a look at your safe."

They all squeezed into Shannon's office, and she opened the safe. The bank bag with the cash Shannon had placed in the safe earlier was still intact, along with folders she stored there.

"Are the papers in those folders important?" Grayson asked.

Shannon nodded. "It's the deed to the store and the artists' leases for the lofts."

"You might want to make copies and put the originals in a safe-deposit box." Grayson rubbed his balding head. "If anyone were to ever take the whole safe—and I've seen it done before—you'd lose it all."

"That's probably wise." Shannon shut the safe door. "I'll do that."

"Would you like us to move the safe back where you had it?"

Shannon glanced around at the room full of men. "That would be wonderful. I doubt Essie and I would have much luck moving it ourselves."

The four men could barely get hold of it at the same time, due to its small size, but when they all managed to get a good grip, it took only a moment for them to set the safe back against the wall in its former position.

Shannon smiled with gratitude. "Thank you so much. Come back during business hours and have a latte on me."

"Thanks." Officer Brownley broke into a goofy grin, revealing his trademark jack-o'-lantern teeth.

Grayson grunted an acknowledgement and switched his focus to Officer Doan. "Did you boys look around upstairs?"

"Yes, sir. Most of the doors are locked, but we checked the rooms we could get in."

"Those are the artists' lofts," Shannon said. "I rent them on a monthly basis, and they each have their own keys."

"Do you have a master key?" Grayson asked.

"Yes."

"Then let's check them. I'd hate to find out later some- one was holed up inside one of them while we were down here daydreaming about foo-foo coffee drinks." He cast a sharp look at Officer Brownley, who seemed to shrink beneath his gaze. "Doan, you stay here and see if there's anything you can secure that back door with. Brownley, come with me."

Alec stepped forward. "I'll help secure the door."

Shannon gave him a wan smile. "Take a look in the storage room. There may be some lumber scraps there."

As she climbed the stairs with the chief and Officer

Brownley, the young officer asked, "Is there a separate entrance to these lofts?"

"Just the fire escape," Shannon said. "This is the only stairway. The artists have to enter through the store."

She unlocked the doors one by one, and the policemen checked each space. When they came to Fredo's door, she paused and looked at the chief. "I found something disturbing in this loft earlier—when I was locking up for the evening."

"Oh?" Grayson's brown eyes glittered with interest.

"This space is rented by an artist named Fredo Benson. When I was closing tonight, I noticed light coming from his loft. I knocked to see if he was in there. Sometimes the artists stay late to work."

"Was he?"

"No. Nobody was here at that time, but Fredo had left a lamp on." She swung the door open and flipped the light switch. "It was the lamp on his desk. I came in to turn it off, and that's when I saw this painting." She pointed to the medium-size canvas displayed on Fredo's easel.

Grayson frowned at it. "I've seen that fountain before."

"Yes, you have." She paused. "It's in the garden in my backyard."

His eyebrows shot up. "Is this Benson fellow a friend of yours?"

"No, just a tenant. As far as I know, he's never been in my house. Seeing this gave me such a start that I ..." She winced, not liking the feeling she got from having to admit she'd snooped—especially to Grayson, of all people. He'd made it quite clear the last time their paths had crossed during one of his investigations that he thought she was a busybody.

"You what?" Grayson demanded.

"I saw Fredo's sketchbook lying there on his desk, and I ... um ..." She looked up at him and felt her face flush.

Grayson sighed. "Let me guess. You looked through it."

"I took a tiny peek."

Grayson's deepening scowl did nothing to diminish her uneasiness about violating another person's privacy. "So let's hear it."

— 3 —

"I found several drawings—all quite creepy, I might add—of my house in Fredo's sketchbook," Shannon said, watching Grayson's steady brown eyes for further reaction. "Some were of the grounds, but one was definitely an interior view. And there's even a detailed sketch of my truck, parked *inside* the garage."

She glanced toward the doorway to make sure Alec hadn't followed them upstairs, but no one had accompanied them except Officer Brownley.

From below, she heard hammering that she hoped meant Alec and Officer Doan were busy barricading the back door. Most likely, they would make a mess of the doorframe, but she'd worry about that later. At the moment, security was paramount.

"Where is the sketchbook now?" Grayson asked.

"It's out in my truck, under the driver's seat. I decided to take it home with me so I could compare some of the sketches to the real thing, to make sure I wasn't leaping to unjustified conclusions."

"But you left it in your truck?"

Shannon shrugged. "I didn't want the kids to see it and get curious. I figured I'd look it over closely in the morning and then bring it back here with me. My plan is to confront Fredo when he comes in. I mean, it's possible he knew my grandmother and visited the house months ago, before I moved here. But I fear that's not the case, and that makes me uneasy."

"I can understand that." Grayson rubbed his chin as if deep in thought. "Do you think it was Fredo who broke in?"

Shannon shook her head. "His creepy sketches aside, I have no reason to suspect him of wanting to rob the store. And although the renters can only access their lofts while the store is open, I don't think any of them would be so desperate to get into their lofts after hours that they would break in."

Grayson nodded. "If we don't find any obvious clues to our burglar's identity soon, we'll talk to all of your renters, just the same. Do you have contact information for all of them?"

"Yes. They should all be in tomorrow if you want to stop by. Some have classes scheduled, and others will come in to work on their art."

"We'll drop by tomorrow during business hours. Can you have a list ready for us in the morning with their addresses and phone numbers? Any who aren't around, we'll track down as needed."

Shannon eyed him skeptically. "You don't seriously think one of my tenants broke in here, do you?"

Grayson shrugged. "It's hard to say. And this thing with the sketches of your house does seem odd, but it may not be sinister. Fredo could have seen photos of the Paisley mansion."

"I suppose it's possible."

"I'll talk to Fredo about it tomorrow. Have that sketchbook handy too. I suspect this burglary was entirely unrelated, a crime of opportunity." The chief smiled at her—

a rare occurrence—and the lines at the corners of his eyes crinkled. "Go home and get some sleep now. I don't expect the thief will be back."

"I hope you're right." They exited Fredo's loft, and Shannon locked the door behind them.

"Would you like an officer to see you home?" Grayson asked as they headed down the stairs.

"No, thanks. Alec's with me; we'll be fine."

A few minutes later, Shannon and Alec climbed back into her old truck. As soon as they pulled away from the store, Alec hit her with a barrage of questions.

"Who exactly is this Frodo Benson guy, Mum?"

"It's Fredo, not Frodo. He's one of the artists who rents a loft. You've seen him, haven't you?"

"Is he the weird bird? The one who cut off part of his ear and thinks he's Van Gogh?"

Shannon clucked her tongue. "That would be Fredo."

"What did you and Chief Grayson find in his loft? You sure spent a lot of time up there."

Shannon shrugged, attempting to appear nonchalant. "Nothing, really. We were just discussing the break-in." She hated to lie, but it was in Alec's best interest. She didn't want to cause him any more stress where her safety was concerned.

"Hmm." Alec clearly wasn't satisfied. "Is Fredo a main suspect?"

"I don't think so."

"Who do you think did it, then?"

"I don't have a clue. I'm sure the chief has a list of 'usual suspects' though."

Alec snorted. "I never would've guessed a small town like Apple Grove would have such a list—or so much crime."

"Neither would I," Shannon shivered, "but there sure has been since *I* arrived."

"True, but I was thinking more along the lines of shop burglaries. We won't even begin to talk about the string of murders you've managed to get mixed up in."

"I wouldn't call it a *string* of murders." Shannon fixed him with a stern look, the glow from a streetlight illuminating her glare. "As a matter of fact, none of the crimes you're referring to were connected."

"OK, fine. You're right. But this burglary seems so odd to me. I mean, why would someone break into a craft shop? Why not a bank, or at least a restaurant or a hotel? They couldn't possibly think you'd have a lot of cash lying around."

"It doesn't make sense, does it?" Shannon frowned and turned to stare out the windshield. Alec was right. Her shop *was* an unlikely target.

"Unless," Alec paused, "they knew you had a safe."

"Most stores have safes."

"All right, scratch that. Perhaps the burglar knew something about your business—that something he wanted was likely to be in there."

Shannon pulled her gaze from the road. "Are you suggesting it was an *employee*?"

"Maybe. Or it could've been one of those artist tenants. Or even one of their students."

Shannon considered the student angle. "It's possible, I guess."

Alec snapped his fingers. "I've got it! Maybe it was a

customer who saw something in your shop and decided to come back after hours and help himself—or herself."

"Really. You think one of my craft customers did this?" Shannon shook her head. "I can't believe that. I know most of them by name. We're a tight little community."

"Crafty people *have* been known to commit crimes." Alec flipped on the turn signal and swung onto the long driveway leading to the mansion.

Shannon noticed the house was still dark except for the light over the front entrance and a dull glow from the sidelights near the door. "I hope Lara slept through all of this."

Alec parked the truck in the garage, and they let themselves in the front door. A small table lamp in the foyer lit their path as they crept toward the stairs.

"Everything all right?" Deborah's voice halted their steps. She appeared in the kitchen hallway, still wrapped in her blue housecoat, her formerly wild hair now tamed.

"Goodness, Deborah, you shouldn't have waited up," Shannon said.

Deborah shrugged. "Couldn't go back to sleep. And you were gone a whole hour, so I figured it was more than a squirrel in the wiring."

"Well, yes." Shannon looked at Alec.

"Somebody smashed in the back door of the shop," he said. "Have we got any biscuits?"

Deborah's mouth quirked in a half smile, but then morphed back into a line. "Did they catch him? And yes, check the cookie jar."

"Thanks." Alec shuffled off to the kitchen, and it fell on Shannon to tell the tale.

"Whoever it was had left by the time the police got there. They messed up my office a little—not bad—but so far I don't think anything was taken. It could have been a lot worse."

Deborah frowned. "You'll have to get that door repaired right away."

"I plan to. One of the officers looked for fingerprints on the doorframe and the safe, but he didn't find—"

"The safe? Land sakes alive!" Deborah clutched her robe so tightly her knuckles turned white. "Did they crack it?"

"Uh—no. It had been moved a short distance, but they must have given up on it. Everything in it appeared to be untouched."

Deborah let out a big sigh. "That's a relief."

"It sure was." Shannon stifled a yawn. "I need to go to bed. So do you. Don't let Alec keep you up."

"Oh, the boy's got to have a midnight snack. He's a good kid."

Shannon smiled. "Yes, he is. I'll see you at breakfast." She trudged up the stairs, wondering if she'd be able to sleep. Once again, she'd left Fredo's sketchbook in the truck. Now she wished she'd brought it in for safekeeping— but she felt too drained to go back outside and retrieve it.

As she lay in bed with the moonlight streaming through her window, she mentally reviewed a list of her loft tenants and employees. *How well do I really know any of them? Would one of them try to rob me?*

She remembered Fredo's creepy drawings and shivered. *Would Fredo?*

*   *   *

On Friday morning, Shannon spent her first hour in the craft market gathering information for the chief. Essie manned the checkout counter and assisted early shoppers while Shannon worked in her office. After Essie's initial shock at the news of the break-in, she'd taken over with a no-nonsense practicality that Shannon admired.

Compiling a list of loft tenants topped Shannon's agenda. She transferred contact information for each of the artists into a computer file. Essie's name appeared first on the list—free loft rental was a benefit of being the assistant manager. Shannon couldn't have asked for a better person for the job. The gifted young woman was talented in many areas, and she'd attracted countless new customers through her classes in beading, drawing, and chalk art.

Shannon included contact information for the other women who worked part-time on an as-needed basis. In a town the size of Apple Grove, she suspected Grayson would know almost everyone on the list. Though one of the artists lived in a neighboring town, it wouldn't take his men long to contact all of the renters.

At ten o'clock, Essie knocked on the open office door.

Shannon swiveled her chair. "What's up?"

Essie smiled apologetically. "Just checking in. Fredo has a painting class scheduled for ten, but he's not here. Three of his students are milling around the shop because his loft isn't open yet."

"Hmm. He's not usually late, is he?" Shannon asked.

"No. On days when he teaches classes, he's here when we open the store."

"OK. I'll call him."

"Already tried," Essie said. "No answer."

Shannon leaned back in her chair, stymied. "Did you call his cellphone? Maybe he's en route."

"I'm pretty sure I called his cell."

"I'll pull up his file and see what numbers we have on record." Shannon turned toward her computer as Essie headed back to the sales floor. She found only one phone number listed for Fredo. Since it wasn't a local exchange, she, too, assumed it was a mobile phone. For good measure, she tried it.

After six rings, the call rolled into Fredo's voice mail. Shannon left a message and hung up. She clicked a few more keys on her computer, shoved back her chair, and grabbed her purse.

Out in the main part of the store, she spotted Essie hanging packets of beading supplies on a spinner display. A couple of women hovered nearby, browsing the merchandise, and three young people stood chatting in the doorway to the coffee shop—likely Fredo's students.

Shannon joined Essie. "I'm going to Fredo's apartment to see if he overslept."

Essie blinked, clearly surprised. "You are?"

Shannon knew it must seem like an odd thing to do. She'd certainly never made a house call for any other artist. But no other artist had ever created paintings and sketches of her home without permission. She intended to talk to Fredo that morning, one way or another.

"If he shows up here, have him get the class going," Shannon instructed. "In the meantime, perhaps you could take his students into the coffee shop and give a quick lesson. Got anything up your sleeve?"

"Um, sure. I don't know what level they're at, but I could do something on perspective."

"That would be wonderful. And if the police stop by while I'm gone, there's a contact list of all our tenants and employees on my desk, waiting for them." The bell above the front door chimed, and Shannon cringed. *The last thing we need is a rush of customers while Essie's here alone this morning.* To her relief, it was only Alec and Lara coming through the door, smiling and full of energy.

"Hi, Mum." Lara grinned and sauntered over to them with Alec trailing behind. "We were wondering when you want to go on that shopping trip to Portland we talked about."

"Oh, I completely forgot. Not today, but soon— I promise." Shannon adjusted her purse on her shoulder. "Right now I've got to go track down one of our artists. Can you stay and help Essie for a few minutes? Cover the coffee counter if it gets too busy?"

Lara gave a mock salute. "You got it."

"Want me to go with you?" Alec's usual sunny demeanor had darkened.

Shannon recognized the look—he was showing his protective streak. *No doubt due to last night's interruption.* "Sure." She turned to Essie and Lara. "We'll be back soon."

She and Alec stepped out into the beautiful Oregon sunshine.

"How did you kids get here?" Shannon asked.

"Biked. We stowed them out back. Want me to drive?"

"I'll drive. You help navigate."

Shannon had a vague idea where Fredo's street was, and

with Alec's help, she soon located the house—a rambling Victorian that had been divided into flats. She parked in front, and they mounted the steps to the covered porch. A list to one side of the main door held cards with the tenants' names and apartment numbers. The bottom one read, "F. BENSON # 4—BACK ENT."

"Looks like we have to go around back." Alec darted off before she could reply.

The porch wrapped around the side of the house, and they followed it, searching for another entrance. At the far end of the porch, Shannon found it, marked with "TAYLOR #3" and "BENSON #4" placards. She pressed the doorbell, and they waited.

After a minute, Alec tried the doorknob.

"Alec!" Shannon hissed. "What are you doing? We can't go in someone's house without permission." Flashing back to her own entry into Fredo's loft, she felt like a hypocrite the moment the words left her mouth.

The door swung open halfway. Alec nudged it farther, revealing a small foyer at the foot of a staircase. A young man of about twenty jogged down the steps toward them, a canvas carryall slung over his shoulder.

"Hello," he called as he hit the bottom step. "Can I help you?"

Shannon stepped forward. "We're here to see Fredo Benson."

"Oh, he's in four."

"Yes, I know. Where is that, exactly?"

The young man nodded toward a door to the left of the staircase. "Right over there."

He was out the front door before Shannon could ask anything else.

She looked at Alec. "Shall we?"

They approached the door with a black numeral "4" stuck on the middle panel, and Shannon knocked. They waited a few seconds, and she eyed Alec anxiously. "What do you think?"

Alec rapped soundly on the door panel, but still they got no response.

"I'll try to call him again." Shannon fumbled in her purse for her phone, but before she had it out, Alec was reaching for the doorknob. "Alec don't!"

It turned without protest, and the door creaked open a few inches.

Shannon lowered her voice to a whisper. "This can't be good."

"Aw, Mum, you watch too many crime shows." Alec pushed open the door far enough to stick his head inside. "Hullo! Anybody home?"

Silence greeted them.

"Should we go in?" he asked.

"Of course not! We shouldn't have even opened the door." Shannon glanced nervously behind her. "I've got a bad feeling about this. Maybe I should call Chief Grayson."

"Just let me take a quick peek first."

Before she could protest, Alec slipped inside.

"Alec, wait." *This child will be the death of me.*

Shannon stepped through the doorway and gazed about the small living area. At first glance, nothing seemed out of the ordinary in the living space or the tiny kitchen area, except for clutter and dust. The coffee table was piled with books, dishes, and a couple of items of clothing. An easel stood in the living room, and Shannon recognized the painting atop it as Van Gogh's *Pink Roses in a Vase*. Knowing Fredo was a Van Gogh fanatic, that didn't surprise her. It certainly wasn't an original; perhaps the eccentric artist had purchased a copy for inspiration. An afghan, two throw pillows, a discarded sweatshirt, and several magazines camouflaged the sofa.

Nothing in the room screamed out to Shannon that she should beware. But her instincts told her something wasn't right. *Surely Fredo isn't enough of a free spirit to leave his doors unlocked all the time.*

"Mum!"

Shannon jerked her head around to meet Alec's horrified gaze. He stood in the doorway to the bedroom, his face ashen beneath his light summer tan.

"What is it?" But she knew, even before he answered.

"Call the chief. I think he's dead."

— 4 —

Shannon and Alec sat in the old Ford pickup and watched as Chief Grayson and three other officers swarmed the apartment building.

"I should have called the police when Fredo didn't answer the door," Shannon said bleakly.

"You had no way of knowing, Mum."

"But after last night …"

Alec reached over and patted her hand. "It's not your fault. We were all a bit on edge because of the burglary. You're not psychic."

"Still … I shouldn't have let you go in there. We may have destroyed important evidence they'll need." She turned to face him, blinking fiercely against hot tears. "I'm sorry, Alec. That was a horrible experience for you."

"Aw, come on. It's not your fault." Her son awkwardly put his arms around her and stroked her shoulder. "You can't blame yourself. And think about it—now I've got another corker of a story to email my friends in Scotland about."

She sat bolt upright. "Oh, no! You mustn't talk about this to anyone. Not unless the chief says you can. They might want to keep things hush-hush while they investigate."

Alec scoffed. "This isn't the telly."

"No, it's real life. I'm telling you, sometimes the police really do hold back information. That way, if they bring someone in for questioning, they can see if he knows about things they didn't reveal to the press."

"Maybe, but that would be weird stuff. I didn't see anything unusual. I mean, just the poor fellow lying there on the bed with ..." Alec grimaced, and his whole body shuddered.

Shannon hugged him, taking her turn at comforting. After all, Alec was the one who would never get the grisly image out of his brain—and she knew that from experience. "I'm so, *so* sorry you had to see that."

Alec's back stiffened beneath her grasp. "It's no big deal."

Shannon sat back with a sigh. "I'd better call the store. Lara and Essie must be wondering where we are."

"Good idea." Alec rolled down his window and peered at the house. A few people had gathered on the sidewalk in front of it, and a uniformed officer stood post on the porch steps.

Shannon took out her phone and dialed the shop.

Lara answered, a little breathless. "Paisley Craft Market & Artist Lofts. May I help you?"

"Sweetie, it's Mum. Just wanted to give you all an update."

"Terrific. It's busy here, and we need you."

"I'll get there as soon as I can. Tell Essie to keep on with the class. Fredo ..." She hesitated. "Well, he won't be in."

"Oh? What's up?"

"I'll tell you everything when we get back, but it may be a little while. Look on my desk, open the address file, and call Carrie Weston. See if she can come in today. And can you stay there awhile? At least until she gets there?"

"Sure, Mum. You sound strange. Is everything OK?"

How does she always know? Shannon let out a long sigh. "Not really. If you can't get Carrie, see if Melanie can help out today." Her voice cracked, and she gritted her teeth. She didn't want to upset Lara, but the strain of the morning's events was catching up to her.

"Will do. Get back soon—I'm *dying* of curiosity."

Shannon cringed at her daughter's choice of words. "Sorry, kiddo. I'll fill you in when we get there, but it may be an hour or so."

As Shannon signed off, Chief Grayson emerged from the house and marched across the lawn toward her truck. He looked exhausted, and his face appeared grayer than usual. Shannon and Alec climbed out of Old Blue and met him halfway.

"Which one of you went in first?" he demanded.

Shannon blinked. *So much for pleasantries.*

"I did, um, sir," Alec said. "Mum didn't see him. I wouldn't let her."

"Good choice." Grayson took a small notebook and pen from his pocket and prepared to write. "How much time elapsed between when you first saw the body and when you called it in?"

"None." Alec glanced at Shannon. "I mean, Mum whipped her phone out as soon as I said I thought he was dead."

Grayson nodded and wrote. "And why exactly did you come over here this morning?"

Shannon cleared her throat. "Fredo had a ten o'clock art class. He didn't show. I tried to phone him, but he didn't answer." She silently prayed Grayson wouldn't mention the strange drawings she'd found in Fredo's sketchbook in front of Alec.

"And that's unusual?"

"Yes. Fredo's always very prompt. In fact, he's usually at the store early, to prepare for his class."

Grayson nodded. "How many students?"

"I'll have to check the roster to see how many are registered, but at least three were there waiting when I left the store. I told Essie to get them started on something while I came over to check on Fredo."

"So they're still at the store now?"

"Should be."

Grayson made another note. "Let's talk about Fredo's apartment. Tell me how things were when you got here."

Shannon glanced at Alec, then plunged in. "We went up on the front porch first, because we didn't know which apartment was his. Then we went around the back and found another entrance. Oh, and it wasn't locked."

"Then what?" Grayson asked.

"Uh …" She frowned, trying to remember everything.

"That guy came down the stairs," Alec said.

The chief focused on Alec. "What guy?"

"I dunno. Some bloke who was coming down when we went in. Mum asked him where Fredo lived, and he pointed to the door next to the stairs. Then he left."

"That's right," Shannon said. "I assumed he was the tenant from the upstairs apartment. He seemed in a hurry."

Grayson tapped his pen on the notepad. "Did he look upset or anxious?"

"No." Shannon shook her head. "He was quite cheerful. And he carried some kind of a knapsack or messenger bag."

"We'll check with the upstairs tenant and make sure it was him that you saw," Grayson said. "Now, when you got to Benson's door—"

"We knocked," Shannon said. "There wasn't any bell."

"No one answered," Alec offered.

Grayson frowned. "So you just walked in?"

Alec's gaze dropped to the ground as though the grass around his shoes had suddenly become very interesting. "Mum was going to try and call him again, but since the other door wasn't locked...."

"Don't tell me, you opened it." Grayson cast an exasperated look at Shannon.

Shannon felt herself bristle. "It's a good thing we did. Who knows how long it might've been before someone found him!"

"It wasn't locked." Alec met the chief's hardened gaze and gave him a sheepish grin. "Sorry. I hope we didn't wreck your investigation."

"Trespassing." Grayson shook his head and muttered something under his breath. "Shannon, I don't know how you manage to do it, but once again, you've gotten yourself mixed up in my case." He eyed them both sternly. "Did you touch anything?"

"Don't think so," Alec said. "The door to the bedroom was wide open. I just popped my head in to see if Fredo was in there." He stopped, suddenly looking a little ill. "And there he was. Well, you saw him."

"Yes." Grayson studied Alec. "It's hard to see someone like that—even for an old-timer like me."

Shannon swallowed hard. "I didn't touch anything except the door, I don't think. I was looking about in the sitting room when Alec told me he'd found Fredo. Then I got my phone out and made the call. The dispatcher told me to go outside and wait for you, so we did. We went straight to the truck."

The chief made a few more scribbles on his notepad and then flipped it shut. "You both can go now, but we may need to talk to you again later. We may require your fingerprints so we can compare them with whatever we find in there."

"Was he shot?" Alec asked.

"That's not your concern. The medical examiner will tell us—the *police*—the cause of death, after the autopsy." Grayson glanced toward the street where a black sedan was pulling up parallel to the sidewalk. "Looks like he's here now. Go on, you two. And the less you talk to folks about this, the better."

"Is it all right if I tell Essie?" Shannon asked.

"If you must, but don't give her details. And whatever you do, don't talk to any reporters. Refer them to me. You got that?" He looked gravely from her to Alec.

"Got it," Alec said.

Shannon nodded. "Thank you."

They climbed into the truck, and Shannon sat quietly for a moment before exhaling a long, deep breath. "You OK?"

Alec kept his eyes on the windshield. "Yeah."

She started to put the key in the ignition, but tears flooded her eyes. She swiped at them with the back of her hand. *If only I'd come alone, Alec would've been spared the grisly sight that will no doubt haunt him for the rest of his life.*

She turned to Alec. "I'm sorry I got you into this."

"Don't beat yourself up. I asked to come." Alec shrugged. "Anyway, it's not that big of a deal. Want me to drive?"

"Maybe." After a moment, she held out the keys to him and opened her door. They switched places, and Alec wove the truck through the congested traffic on the residential street. In five minutes, they were back at the craft store.

Dismayed, Shannon stared at the building. "I'll have to tell Lara and Essie."

"I can stay and help with the store."

She shook her head. "If Essie managed to get someone else to come in, it might be better if you took Lara home. The police will be in and out all day, and people will talk. I'd like to know your sister's not in the middle of it all—like she was when Alton Percy died."

She hesitated while Alec got out of the truck. As soon as he closed the door, she bent down and groped under the driver's seat. Her fingers closed on the spine of Fredo's sketchbook, and she pulled it onto her lap. She should have put it in a bag. Now her fingerprints were all over it.

Alec stood waiting for her on the sidewalk. His gaze zeroed in on the book as she climbed out of the truck. "What's that?"

"Oh, it's nothing. Come on."

She forced herself to smile as they entered the store, hoping he'd forget about the sketchbook.

Surveying the store, she spotted Lara behind the checkout counter, while Carrie, one of the part-time helpers, assisted a customer in the bead section. From the coffee shop, Shannon heard Essie's cheerful voice instructing a class.

"Is that still the 10 a.m. class?" Shannon asked Lara, glancing at her watch. To her surprise, it was nearly eleven o'clock.

"Yes. They're about ready to wind it up, I think. A salesman stopped by looking for you earlier," Lara said, rolling her eyes, "but when I told him you weren't here, he said he'd come back later and he left."

"Oh, joy."

Lara leaned forward on the counter. "So what's up with Fredo? The suspense is killing me."

Shannon glanced at Alec. "I'll let Alec take you home and tell you. Keep the information to yourself. You can talk to Deborah about it, but nobody else, OK?"

Lara's eyes widened. "That bad?"

"I'll say." Alec pulled a grim face. "Come on, let's get our bikes."

"Why don't you drive?" Shannon held out the keys to him. "Put the bikes in the back. I'll call you when I'm ready to come home."

Alec didn't protest. Lara grabbed her woven purse and hurried out the back door with him, calling, "Bye, Mum."

A moment later, Carrie and her customer approached the checkout counter.

"Hi," Carrie said. "I can ring this up."

"Great." Shannon stepped aside. "When Essie's class is dismissed, would you both come see me for a moment in my office, please? I want to catch you up on a couple of things."

"Sure."

Shannon walked to her office and locked her purse and the sketchbook in the file drawer. She realized she'd left the door to the room wide open, and it hit her anew how easy it would be for anyone to sneak in when the clerks weren't looking, to rifle her desk and files. How trusting she was— all of them were, really.

She grabbed her big batch of keys and headed for the stairs. One thing was for certain: She intended to keep Fredo's loft locked for the short term. *Thank goodness I asked Essie to take his students into the coffee shop, instead of up to his loft where they might've destroyed evidence.*

She tried the doorknob to his loft and found it locked. Satisfied, she trudged down the steps, her mental to-do list growing by the minute. She needed to let all the students know that the rest of Fredo's class sessions were canceled. Maybe she should do that as they left today—but no, Chief Grayson had said not to publicize Fredo's death yet. Better to wait until things calmed down and then call them individually.

Calm. Shannon tried not to laugh as the word floated through her mind. *I haven't had a calm moment since I moved to Apple Grove.*

— 5 —

Officer Brownley stopped by the store shortly after noon to pick up the contact lists Shannon had prepared.

"I'm afraid all of Fredo's students from this morning's class have left," she told him.

He glanced at the top sheet of paper. "Looks like a small class."

"Yes, only five. Will you be talking to them today, or should we let them know the rest of the class sessions are canceled?"

"I'll try to talk to them this afternoon." He tucked the papers under his arm. "I'll have them call the store if they have questions about the classes."

"That's fine. And I meant what I said earlier about the free latte—or any drink of your choice. Why don't you order something for the road? On me."

He grinned. "Thanks."

After Officer Brownley left, business slowed down, so she called Essie and Carrie over near the cash register to break the news that Fredo had died.

Carrie's jaw dropped. "No."

"What happened?" Essie cried.

"We don't know. We walked in and found him—that is, Alec found him. The police will have to sort it out. I'm staying out of it, and I'm staying out of Grayson's way."

Essie raised her brows, clearly unconvinced.

"Really." Shannon nodded for emphasis. "I'm not getting any more involved in this mess than I have to."

"Does this have anything to do with the burglary last night?" Essie asked. "I was still stressing about that, and now we're hit with this."

"I hope not." Shannon grimaced. "I don't see how it would, but still ..."

Carrie leaned in. "Do you know how he died?"

"No, I don't."

Two women entered the store, and Shannon sent Carrie and Essie back to work. She continued to mull over Essie's question. *Is the timing of the two events, so close together in occurrence, purely a coincidence?* Both crimes had a strong connection to her store. But Fredo's death might not have been a crime at all. How would the coroner classify it? Natural causes? Accident? Suicide? Or would they have to go through the trauma of another murder investigation?

Alec had asked the chief if Fredo had been shot. *Maybe there was a lot of blood at the scene.* She'd avoided talking about the details with her son for fear of upsetting him further. She decided that for now, she was happy not knowing.

A man walked through the front door, and she thought at first that the salesman had returned. But his work clothes didn't fit those of a polished salesperson. He strode toward her and said, "Hi. Someone called about a repair job. I'm here to give you an estimate."

Shannon had almost forgotten about the damage to the back entrance.

"I called. Let me show you the damage." She led him

down the hallway and unlocked the back door so he could examine both sides of the doorframe. "I'll be right there in my office when you're done."

About ten minutes later, he handed Shannon an estimate to give to her insurance company. "I can come back tomorrow with the materials, if you want."

"Thank you." She quickly glanced over his numbers. "I'll contact my insurance carrier right away and let you know."

She made the call and managed to set up the repair job without any snags. At one o'clock, she ran over to The Apple Grove Inn for a sandwich, rather than asking Alec to come get her for lunch. Traffic in the store was fairly slow after that, so she sent Carrie home. She dealt with the salesman, and at quarter past three, Chief Grayson walked in. If possible, he looked wearier—and grumpier—than he had that morning.

"Hello, Shannon. Can I talk to you in private?"

"Of course." Shannon led Grayson to the office. She sank down in her desk chair and waved Grayson to another seat near the file cabinet. "So what can you tell me about Fredo?"

Grayson opened his mouth to speak and then closed it, eyeing her suspiciously.

She held up her hands in mock surrender. "I'm only asking as a concerned citizen and business owner. I'm not trying to solve your case."

He chuckled. "I ought to get that on tape." He leaned back in his chair, eliciting a groan from the delicate wood. "Looks like a homicide."

Shannon sighed. "I was hoping you wouldn't say that. Not that I'd hoped he'd killed himself, but Fredo *was* an odd fellow. He thought highly of himself as an artist, but he was very temperamental. I wouldn't have been shocked if you said he did himself in."

"Well, we didn't find a weapon, and one was obviously used. I'd say he was struck with a blunt instrument, but I don't know what. I'm hoping the coroner's report will tell us more."

"And Alec saw him." Shannon felt queasy. *I didn't protect my son.*

"It … wasn't as bad as it might have been," Grayson said gently. "Tell me what you meant when you said Fredo was temperamental."

She shrugged. "He was fussy about his space, and he acted like a prima donna. Seemed to think he should get preferential treatment over the other tenants. For instance, I bought four fans last week—you know how hot it was. Even with the AC going full blast—which cost a fortune—those lofts get pretty warm. I saw some on sale, and I bought all that the store had in stock. I gave them out on a first-come, first-serve basis. Well, Fredo wasn't here when I brought them in, so he didn't get one. When he found out later, he was angry and demanded that I take one away from another artist and give it to him." She raised her hands in defeat. "I wound up making a special trip to another store and buying a fan just for Fredo."

"Sounds like a high-maintenance renter."

"The highest. But he's also very good at what he does, and his students love him. He has a gift for teaching—or I should say he *had* one." She paused. "I think he seemed a bit lofty to them, and maybe a little mysterious. He wasn't always easy to please, but that's good in a teacher sometimes."

Grayson made a note. "He had an old wound that was pretty much healed over on his left ear. Do you know how he got that?"

"I can only tell you what he *said*."

Grayson arched an eyebrow.

Shannon continued, "He told us he'd cut off his earlobe to honor his favorite painter."

"Van Gogh?"

She nodded.

Grayson looked a little skeptical, but he jotted it down. "We took his cellphone and computer to see if we can get any clues from those. We'll need to go over his loft space more thoroughly."

"Of course. I'll give you the key." She swiveled her chair around to rummage through a drawer.

"Shannon, there's one more thing."

Something in his tone put her on the alert. Her pulse picked up as she spun to face him again. "What is it?"

"On his phone, we found several photos of your house."

Shannon stopped breathing for a moment. She shouldn't be shocked, not after the sketches in his loft. *But photos?* Things were closing in on her, making it hard to inhale. "I ... see."

"I'd like to compare them with the drawings you found earlier," Grayson said.

"All right. I brought the sketchbook in with me this morning. The painting of the garden is in his loft." Slowly she rose from her chair, making certain her rubbery legs would support her. Then she walked to the file cabinet and pulled the sketchbook from a drawer. "I'm sorry I handled it so much. My fingerprints are all over it."

"I'm not worried about that as far as this item's concerned." Grayson took it and leafed casually through the first few pages. He stopped and studied one picture for a long moment.

"What is it?" Shannon asked.

"This drawing is similar to one of the photos on Fredo's phone."

"Inside or outside?"

He didn't answer.

Shannon stood and peered over his shoulder. "Oh." She swallowed hard. "So this is proof. He was inside my house. Wonderful." Even in a rough sketch, the equestrian statue was impressive.

"He had to be, to get that shot on his camera." Grayson flipped the page. "We're checking all the date stamps on the pictures."

"And?"

"I hate to tell you this, but Fredo was in your home more than once."

Shannon felt the blood drain from her face, and she plopped down into her chair. "When?" *Please tell me it was before Victoria died.*

"The most recent photos were taken last week."

"*Last week?*" She sat up straight, eyes wide. "But we've been there—the kids—Deborah." She puffed out a breath and shook her head. "Unbelievable!"

"I'm sorry." Grayson closed the sketchbook. "Do you always keep the alarm set?"

"Not as often as we should. I usually activate it when I get home in the evening. We'll be more careful about setting it now, I can assure you."

"That's probably a good idea." Grayson rubbed his shiny forehead. "With your track record of getting mixed up in bizarre crimes ..."

Shannon gritted her teeth. She didn't like the accusatory tone in the chief's statement, but she refused to be drawn into an argument with him. "Are you saying Fredo may have sneaked in during the day, when the doors weren't locked? When we were *in* the house?"

"It's possible. How often do you all go out back to the summer house or the lake?"

"Good point. We've eaten on the patio a lot this summer, and sometimes Deborah goes out to the garden. I doubt she locks up when she does that." Shannon gazed at him, trying to sort her thoughts. "What does this mean? Was he stalking me?"

"It's hard to say." Grayson sighed. "There aren't any pictures of you. Just your environment, so to speak."

"If he were stalking me ... well, he's dead now. No consolation, really." She frowned, unable to make sense of it. "If you want to go to the house and look at the real things—the models—that's fine. I can call Deborah and tell her to expect you."

"Thanks. We may want to do that, but not immediately."

"I understand. This is all tangential to the murder. I'm sure that's your priority now."

"Yes, it is. Do you know of anyone who was angry with Benson?"

Shannon thought for a moment. "No, not really. He had little spats with other people. As I told you, he wasn't the easiest person to get along with. Self-centered. Arrogant. But I can't imagine any of our tenants wanting to kill him."

"His students loved him, you say?"

"*Loved* is a bit strong. They admired him, I think. He was a good artist, and his eccentricities made him a fun and exciting teacher. And he was talented. Several students told me they were learning a lot in his classes."

Grayson made a few more notes. After a minute, he put the notebook away and stood. "I'll take this sketchbook and give it to our tech man for comparison. You be careful, Shannon. I think your plan to let us handle this case without interfer—er, *helping*—is a good one. Make sure you keep your alarm system activated—whether you're at home or not."

Shannon felt her lips twitch at his near slip. "We will. I appreciate your concern."

"Tell Deborah and the kids too."

She accompanied him into the hall. As she watched the chief walk through the store and out the front door, Shannon fought the impulse to run after him and pepper him with more questions. She wanted answers. But she knew him well enough by now to realize he'd play it close to the vest, even with the major players. *It makes no difference anyway. I'm not getting any more involved than I have to—for the kids' sake.*

6

Shannon locked her office door and joined Essie on the sales floor. As she went about routine chores—assisting customers, arranging stock, and ringing up purchases—unanswered questions bombarded her mind. *Who killed Fredo? Is his death related to his forays into the Paisley mansion? And what about the break-in at the store—was Fredo involved in that too?*

She was relieved when five o'clock finally came and Essie flipped the "Open" sign to "Closed." When the last customer left, Shannon sagged onto the stool behind the checkout.

Essie leaned on the counter across from her. "Are you OK?"

Shannon nodded.

"Anything new from the chief?" Essie asked.

"Not really. Why don't you head home? I'll call Alec to come get me. I can vacuum the carpet while I wait for him."

"I'll wait with you. You still need to cash out."

Shannon slapped her forehead. "I totally forgot. You can see how rattled I am." She opened the cash drawer and took out the day's receipts.

She heard the vacuum humming as she sat down in her office to count the money and make the deposit slip for the next day's bank run. When she'd finished and put the bank bag in the safe, she made a quick call to the house, and the housekeeper answered.

"You ready to come home?" Deborah asked.

"I will be by the time Alec can get here."

"I'll tell him. Dinner will be waiting."

Shannon hesitated. "I suppose he told you about the murder."

"Yes. We're keeping the front door locked and the alarm set, so ring when you get here."

Shannon hung up feeling a little more secure. After taking out her handbag and Essie's, she locked her office and returned to the sales floor to find Essie winding up the vacuum cord.

Shannon took a deep breath. Essie was one person she knew could be trusted, and the more Essie knew, the safer she would be. Shannon wanted her to be alert. Essie often opened the store in the morning or cashed out at night. It made sense for her most reliable employee to know the details of the situation.

"Essie, I didn't want to say anything with other people around, but something else happened that's connected to Fredo."

"Oh?"

"I've learned he's been sneaking into my house."

"What? No!" Essie closed the distance between them and drew Shannon into a hug. "You poor thing! When did this happen?"

Shannon poured out the whole story to her friend, sparing no creepy detail.

"This is unreal." Essie shook her head. "But you had no

idea he'd been in the house until you saw his drawings?"

"That's right."

Essie thought for a moment. "Then it seems to me that he wasn't the one who broke in here. I mean, Fredo got into your house without you ever knowing it. Why would he smash open a door here?"

"You're right. He's too clever for that. He would've found a way to get a key."

"I'd think so. It wouldn't be that hard."

Shannon gave her friend a weak smile. "Thanks for the perspective."

"You're welcome. I don't know if it's any comfort or not."

"I'm not sure how much to tell the kids," Shannon confessed. "I don't want to scare them unnecessarily, but I want them to be safe."

Someone rapped on the glass door, and they both jumped at the sound.

"Oh, look," Essie said. "Alec's already here."

Shannon sighed and picked up her things. "Now to face the kids and Deborah. I hate to have to tell them about this, but I need to so they'll be on guard. I'll see you in the morning, Essie."

*　*　*

Shannon opened the *Apple Grove News* at breakfast on Saturday morning, dreading the headlines. To her relief, the story of Fredo's death appeared below the fold on the front page, and the brief article reported it as an "unattended death." She and Alec weren't mentioned, except with a vague "A friend visiting Benson's apartment found him dead Friday morning." The reporter quoted Chief Grayson as saying his department would conduct a full investigation. No doubt Monday's paper would carry an update, reclassifying the death as a homicide. It didn't really make much difference—the whole town would be talking about it all weekend.

She headed to the store expecting business as usual. Lara went along to tend the coffee shop counter, typically busy on Saturdays. Residents of Apple Grove and surrounding towns liked to browse the shop, and tourists often stopped in on their way to the shore. Students filed in and out all day long to attend one of the several arts-and-crafts classes offered.

Shannon smiled when she felt a light drizzle hit her skin as she and Lara dashed into the shop—rainy days were especially good for business at the Paisley Craft Market & Artist Lofts.

A few art students and customers mentioned the news item, and one or two asked questions, but no one pressed the issue. Shannon was glad. She stayed in the checkout area while Essie taught her beading class and one of the other artists, Twila Eaton, held a session in her loft on painting with acrylics. The forty-three-year-old artist had a style all her own, specializing in bold, colorful floral subjects that looked almost like graphic posters. She regularly displayed her canvases in galleries in Astoria and Seaside, and many people seemed to find her bright paintings uplifting.

After she'd dismissed her class, Twila approached Shannon with a pained expression on her face. "I just heard about Fredo. Guess that's what I get for not reading the paper." She eyed Shannon over the top of her cranberry-colored eyeglass frames. "Do you know how he died?"

"No. I don't know any details."

"He was a talented painter." Twila sighed. "I thought he was an interesting addition to our little enclave. But I guess we'll have someone new in there before long, and Fredo will be nothing but a memory."

Shannon blinked with surprise. The way Twila sing-songed her words when talking about Fredo's demise made her sound almost ... cheerful. "I'm not sure when we'll have a new renter in the loft."

"Oh well, life goes on." Twila floated toward the stairway, her lean body swaying and her pale blond hair bouncing a little. She pivoted with her hand on the railing. "By the way, I'm going to put out a sign-up sheet for a new fall class soon."

"Have you set the day and time yet?" Shannon asked.

"Hmm, no. Guess I need to do that." Twila drifted up the stairs, and Shannon went back to work. *Surely Twila didn't have anything to do with Fredo's death.* All of her artists had distinct personalities. Twila existed in her own sphere, coming out of her bubble occasionally and then going back into her usual mode—intense, all-day painting sprees. Shannon gave herself a mental shake. *Not Twila.*

The police kept a low profile that morning, at least so far as the store was concerned. Chief Grayson called Shannon after lunch to assure her they were looking for suspects in her burglary, though Fredo's murder demanded most of their attention.

"Also, I learned a safe was stolen in Seaside in June,"

he said. "I talked to the police chief there, to see if your break-in sounded similar."

"What do you think?"

"That safe was taken from a home, not a store. The thieves carried it several miles away and then blew it open. I'm thinking they probably weren't the same people who tried to take yours, but there's really no way to tell. Anyway, I've put out feelers for leads on burglars who target safes. Something else may turn up."

"Thank you. I appreciate it," Shannon said.

"Mm. Well, you and the kids be on alert, especially when you go home at night. The last person out of the store is the most vulnerable, and so is a resident approaching her home. You're a magnet for trouble, Shannon."

She felt her temper flare. *Is the chief deliberately trying to get a rise out of me?* "I'll keep that in mind."

After she hung up, she found herself watching the front door, eyeing customers with suspicion as they came and went. Shannon didn't want to think ill of her clients, but she couldn't help her uneasiness.

Most of her clientele were repeat customers, and she knew a lot of them by sight, but when an unfamiliar man entered and looked around, wandering between the aisles and darting glances toward the back of the store, her stomach roiled. *Is he casing the place?*

Shannon approached him and forced a smile. "May I help you, sir?"

He didn't return the smile. "My wife is doing some bead-work, and she asked me to get her a special needle for it."

"Of course. Follow me, and I'll show you where they're at."

Shannon walked toward the wall display of crafting needles, and the man trailed behind. "Did she say what size?"

The man gestured at the display. "Um, that one."

"Which one?"

"Size twelve, magnetic." He shifted his weight from foot to foot as though ready to bolt from the store.

Fighting to control her unease at the man's strange behavior, Shannon took the hanging card off the display. "Anything else?"

"No, that's it." He paused, his gruff demeanor softening slightly. "Except that she loves this place."

Shannon blinked. "Oh, how nice. What's her name?"

"Lily. She would have come herself, but she sprained her ankle last week, parasailing."

"That's too bad. I hope she's not in too much pain." She put the needle package and sales slip in a small bag and handed it to him.

"I don't think so. But she's read through a stack of paperbacks, and now she's on this beading kick."

Shannon laughed, feeling her tension ease. "Well, here. Take her this flyer. It advertises our specials for next week. Maybe she'll feel well enough to come in then." She tucked the flyer into his bag, wondering if she'd recognize the woman when she came into the store. "Please give Lily my best."

She watched the man climb into his car and drive away. *I have to stop being so suspicious of everyone.*

Before she could leave the counter, the bell above the door chimed, and a tall figure walked in.

Shannon felt a smile creep across her face at the sight of Michael Stone. "Hello, stranger." She hadn't seen Michael much over the previous month, but whenever she did, her day always seemed a bit more interesting. As co-owner of Stone & McCrary, a security-consulting firm, and as a former Portland police detective, he took a special interest in the crime in his hometown of Apple Grove.

His blue eyes lit when he met her gaze, and he strode toward her. "I heard what happened. Are you all right?"

She nodded. "I'm fine, but thanks for asking. It's nice to see you."

He raked a hand through his dark hair. "I've been out of the country for a week, and I just heard the news from Grayson. It sounds like you've had a busy time of it—again."

"Yes, we have."

He glanced around at the customers in the store. "This murder ..." Michael turned back to Shannon. "Grayson said you and Alec found the body."

"Unfortunately, yes."

"Is Alec handling it OK?"

"He seems to be, but I know it must weigh heavily on his mind. I didn't see him this morning before I left—I figured if he was still asleep, that was a good thing."

"Yes." Michael hesitated. "Would you object to me talking to him?"

"About ... the murder?"

"How he's coping with everything. Sometimes a man will say things to another man that he wouldn't to his mother."

"You mean, if it's giving him nightmares, things like that?"

Michael shrugged. "You never know."

"I think it would be very nice of you to have a chat with

him, whatever the reason, but I suspect you're right. Alec had enough on his plate struggling with adulthood, culture shock, a new home—now this. Thank you."

"Not a problem. I can swing by your place this afternoon, if you think he'll be in."

"I expect he will be."

He stood awkwardly for a moment, as though unsure of what to say next. Several people entered the store, chatting and laughing. Shannon glanced at the clock. The appliqué class was about to begin.

Michael leaned toward her and lowered his voice. "I'll be in town for a few days. Will I see you at church tomorrow?"

She felt her heart skip a beat. "I plan to be there."

His lips parted as though he had more to say, but then he closed them and nodded. "Good. Let me know if you need anything."

Shannon smiled, remembering the desperate situation he'd helped her out of not so long ago. "Thank you. But I'm letting the police handle this one."

He arched a brow.

She laughed. "Honestly. Well, I mean, that's honestly my *plan*."

"Mm-hm. Probably for the best." He held her gaze for a moment. "I'd better go. Your store is getting busy."

Shannon felt her spirit wilt a little. "OK."

"I'll see you tomorrow." Michael nodded to a customer approaching the counter and headed for the door.

Shannon's chest tightened as she gazed after him. Michael seemed to blow hot and cold when it came to her. She'd thought for a moment he might ask her out. *Foolish.*

She probably wasn't ready for a new relationship anyway—at least, she kept telling herself that. Maybe she held
too much of John in her heart. Still, more than three years
had passed since her husband's death. Perhaps she simply
didn't want to loosen her heartstrings until she was sure the
man in question was serious. And Michael Stone could be
very hard to read.

She smiled at the waiting customer. "Hello, Jean. Did
you find everything you were looking for?"

"I think so, except that I was hoping to match this fingering yarn."

"Let me help you search." Shannon accompanied
the customer to the yarn display on the far wall, but her
thoughts kept drifting back to Michael.

— 7 —

Shannon didn't say anything to Alec when she got home that evening about Michael's plan to speak with him, but he brought up the subject over dinner.

"Mr. Stone came by today."

"Oh? He dropped in at the store today too." Shannon passed Alec the plate of garlic bread.

"We took the rowboat out on the lake after the rain stopped." Alec took two pieces of bread before passing it on.

"How nice." Shannon looked across the table at Lara. "Did you go too?"

"Nah, I was chatting online with my friends back home."

"Oh. How is everyone?"

"They're all excited about fall term opening and getting ready for that. It made me feel a little sad not to be there with them, but I think Portland's going to be fun."

"Me too," Alec said. "It'll be an adventure. And if we hate it, we can always go back to St. Andrews next year."

Shannon's heart clenched at the thought. *Please let them love Portland.* He said nothing more about his time with Michael, and Shannon let it rest. The last thing she wanted was for Alec to think she was worried about him.

The next morning, she dressed for church with a little more care than usual, and then she chided herself. *So Michael said he would be there; why should that make a difference in what shoes I wear?* But it did somehow.

He didn't sit with them during the worship service, but afterward, he waited for them outside at the bottom of the church steps, his black hair glistening in the sun.

Shannon waved. "Hello, Michael. Isn't it a beautiful day?"

"It sure is."

"Better than yesterday." She carefully descended the stairs, wishing with every wobbly step that she'd chosen to wear sensible flats instead of her three-inch heels. Once safely on level ground, she tilted her face up to maintain the eye contact.

Alec and Lara slipped past them to talk to a couple of friends on the lawn.

Michael watched them pass, and then he edged closer to Shannon. "Your son's a good kid."

"Thanks." Shannon's heart warmed at the compliment. "Do you think he's handling Friday's trauma all right?"

"He acts a little philosophical about it, but yeah. He's got a good head on his shoulders. My advice is to let it sit another day or two and then ask him if he wants to talk about it. He might, by then. Or not."

"I'll do that," Shannon said. "Thanks again for talking to him."

Deborah sped past them—probably hoping to beat everyone home and take the pot roast and baked potatoes out of the oven.

"Any time. And Shannon, if there's anything else I can do ..." His gaze bored into hers, holding her captive for a moment.

She gave herself a mental shake. "I appreciate it. Depending on what Chief Grayson tells me when he's finished his investigation, I may ask you to look over my security systems again."

A muscle flexed in his jaw. "Grayson mentioned Fredo had been in your house."

"Yes. That worries me more than the store break-in."

"Me too." Michael's eyes shone with sympathy.

"We had no clue he'd been in the house. What I'd like to know is, *how* did he get in? But now that he's dead, we may never know."

"Is there a chance he might have discovered your alarm codes somehow?"

"Highly unlikely. I don't keep the codes for the house at the store. But it makes me wonder if he sneaked in while we were there—or maybe while Deborah was there alone—and one of the doors wasn't locked."

Michael huffed out a breath. "It's got me wondering too. Grayson said he wants me to go with his men when they investigate it. Of course, they've put the murder scene at top priority right now, but I know they'll want to check into any possible connection with Fredo's break-in at your house. It happened so soon before the murder—that might not be a coincidence."

"I'll be glad when they *do* look into it. You're welcome to come with them." A sudden thought struck her. "You know, if Fredo did sneak in one time when a door was unlocked, it's possible he could have found the alarm code hidden in my desk at that time. Then he'd have had access whenever he wanted."

"Maybe," Michael said. "I suggest you change your code."

Out of the corner of her eye, Shannon saw Alec sauntering toward Old Blue.

Michael cleared his throat. "Aside from everything going on with Fredo, has business been good at the store?"

Shannon tapped her chin playfully. "Let's see, other than one of my artists drawing creepy pictures of my home and then mysteriously being murdered ... it's actually been great." She smiled. "The new coffee shop draws in far more people than I expected. It seems like I'm busy all the time these days."

"Opening Espresso Yourself was a great idea. You're clearly a natural at marketing."

Shannon felt herself blush. "If I didn't know better, I'd think you were trying to sweet-talk me into a free drink."

Michael chuckled. "Not at all. But you know what they say about all work and no play. You have to leave a little room in your schedule for fun." He shifted his weight from one leg to the other. "Speaking of that, when's the last time you—"

"Mum!"

Shannon turned to see Lara break away from her friend Missy Thompson. Her daughter placed both hands on her stomach and assumed a pained expression. "Starving," she mouthed.

"I guess the kids are ready for lunch," she told Michael. "I'd better get going. Hungry teenagers can be almost as frightening as sneaky burglars."

Michael smiled a lopsided grin, and a dimple appeared on one cheek. "Sure. Talk to you later."

Shannon and Lara climbed into the old truck where Alec already sat waiting for them behind the wheel.

"Think you'll ever get a newer vehicle?" Lara asked as Shannon squeezed in beside her on the bench seat.

"Maybe, when Old Blue gives up the ghost."

Alec put the transmission in low gear and eased out onto the street.

It hit Shannon suddenly that it wouldn't be much longer before the twins would be leaving Apple Grove. She'd probably get to see them on weekends—Portland wasn't that far. But still ... she'd known it was coming, but their parting had always hovered in the distant future.

"I'm really going to miss you two!" she blurted. Tears pooled in her eyes, and she blinked at them.

"Aw, Mum, we'll miss you too." Lara slid her arm about Shannon's shoulders and gave her a big squeeze. "But anytime you're feeling blue, you can jump in this old clunker and come see us."

Shannon let out a small chuckle. "In that case, you'd better clear out a corner in your dorm room. I might have to move in."

* * *

"You think more than one person was involved in the break-in?" Essie's brown eyes were huge as she listened to Chief Grayson's report the next morning at the store.

Grayson nodded. "I don't think one person alone could have moved that safe even as far as they did. No sane person would even try by himself."

"Do you think it's possible ...?" Shannon let it trail off, but Grayson wasn't about to let her get away with that.

"What are you thinking?"

She shrugged. "That maybe Fredo was the second thief."

"The thought had occurred to me," Grayson said. "In

that case, they might have gone back to his apartment after their unsuccessful attempt here, and his partner killed him then. But it won't work."

"Why not?" Shannon asked.

"I don't want you ladies broadcasting this, but I heard from the coroner's office this morning. They're pretty sure Fredo was dead before the alarm went off here at the store."

Shannon caught her breath. "You mean, that night while we were here looking at the damage—when I showed you the painting in Fredo's loft—he was already dead?"

Grayson nodded. "Coroner says he was dead by nine o'clock that evening."

"The security company called me at one in the morning," Shannon said bleakly.

"That's right. The alarm sounded at their switchboard a few minutes before one."

Essie gulped. "So what happens now, Chief?"

Grayson ran a hand through his short, thinning hair. "Right now we're looking into Benson's personal life. We'll be talking to any friends and relatives we can dig up. I thought I'd talk to any of your artist tenants who are here this morning." He eyed the two of them for a moment. "Can either of you think of someone who might be classified as Fredo's enemy? You said his students liked him."

"They did," Shannon said, "but he could tick people off without trying."

Essie nodded. "That's right. Several of the other renters were put out with him over little things. Even Carrie had a run-in with him one day. He came downstairs and took something without asking her to put it on his tab."

"I remember that day," Shannon said. "Carrie was very upset when she told me about it. She wondered if he'd done it other times. Frankly, I wondered that myself. I put him on notice that he needed to pay for any future supplies he took from the store."

Grayson took out his notebook and wrote in it. "Can you get me a list of all Fredo's art students?"

"They usually kept their own records on their classes," Shannon said. "I keep a schedule of the class times, but the artists take down the sign-up sheets when the sessions start, and they collect the payments themselves."

"Maybe we'll find something in his computer." Grayson made another note. "I'll check with our tech guy on that."

"I could give you the names of several of his pupils," Essie said. "In fact, I gave Officer Brownley the names of the ones who were here last Friday. But Fredo has another group that comes on Tuesdays for a watercolor class, and a Wednesday evening session on model drawing."

Grayson sighed. "Anything you can get me would be appreciated."

Two customers entered the store, a mother and daughter who often shopped for beading supplies, and Essie excused herself to wait on them.

"Listen," Grayson said in a low tone to Shannon, "we've learned that Benson had a criminal record."

She gulped. "Really?"

"That's right. Could we step into your office and talk in private?"

"Sure." She led the way to her office. Once inside, she shut the door and spun around to face Grayson. "I *do* screen the people I rent to, not as thoroughly as I do my employees—"

He held up a hand. "No need to be defensive here. It happens. I'm not saying you did anything wrong, but you should be more thorough in your checks—for your own safety," he said. "What I came to tell you is that I learned a couple of men who were incarcerated at the same time as Fredo—and in the same facility—are out of jail now."

Shannon blinked. "Potential partners in crime?"

"Exactly." He eyed her solemnly. "We'll check into it further. Keep it to yourself for now, OK?"

It struck Shannon that Grayson was being unusually forthcoming with information about the case, a behavior he'd never shown toward her before. Showing up at the store to tell her about possible leads was *not* his typical modus operandi. In the past, getting any information out of him had been like trying to squeeze blood from a turnip.

"I'll keep it to myself," she said. "You don't think they'd come here, do you?"

"I don't know. I'd think they'd stay away from Apple Grove, now that Fredo's dead, but I guess that might depend on whether they were in on what happened the other night."

"They didn't get much, if anything." Shannon glanced around her office. She didn't generally leave valuables in the room—aside from what she kept in the safe. "Do you really think the same thieves would break in here again? They must have seen that we don't leave money lying around."

"All you can do is be cautious. At this point, we don't know if Fredo's jail mates were anywhere near here. It's just a lead to follow up on."

"Do you have pictures of them?" Shannon asked. "I'd

like to know what they look like in case they show up here."

"I'll email you their mug shots. I'm checking with their parole officers now to see where they are and what they're up to. If we learn that Fredo has been in contact with either of them, or that they've been in Apple Grove, that could be very telling."

"What about Fredo's loft?" Shannon asked.

"I'm sorry we haven't gotten to it—so much happened over the weekend. But I'll try to send a couple of people out this afternoon. They need to search his space thoroughly. If he's been up to his old tricks, maybe we'll find some evidence up there. Don't let anybody in the room until we give you the all clear."

She nodded. "If I may ask, what did he do that put him in jail?"

"I'm surprised it got past you." Grayson shook his head. "He was convicted of art forgery."

8

Alec and Lara met Shannon in the garage when she drove home for lunch the next day. Her guilty conscience told her she should be making more of an effort to spend time with them before they left for school. But Grayson had emailed her the mug shots of Fredo's cronies that morning, and she'd spent her free moments studying them, trying to recall if she'd seen them in the store recently.

"Mum, the university people called." Alec reached for the two grocery sacks she carried. "They want to know when we're coming for the campus tour."

Shannon let him take the sacks and frowned. "I'm sorry. It slipped my mind. But we need to do it soon."

"They said tomorrow would be fine." Lara looked at her expectantly.

'Tomorrow?" Shannon hit the button to close the garage door, recalling Grayson's instructions not to leave any doors open to tempt thieves. "Well, I suppose so. We shouldn't put it off much longer."

"No, we shouldn't," Alec said. "We have to move into the dorm on the nineteenth."

"That's less than two weeks away," Lara added, as if Shannon couldn't figure that out.

"All right." She held up both hands. "Let me get washed up. We'll talk about it over lunch."

As she freshened up, Shannon tried not to think about how chaotic her life had suddenly become. Since the break-in at the store and Fredo's death, she'd dealt with the numerous complications those events had caused. She hadn't had time to work on her silversmithing, or finish the antique beaded bag she'd agreed to restore for a client. But the college trip was important, and the kids were right—they needed to do it as soon as possible.

She arrived at the dining table just as Deborah set a covered dish on a trivet. "Whatever that is, it smells wonderful, Deborah."

Before Shannon could sit down, Lara appeared at her side and placed a pad and pen beside her plate. "Thought you might want to make a list of things we need to do before school starts, Mum."

"Thank you. That will be helpful."

They all took a seat as the twins bombarded her with suggestions, and Shannon took notes between bites of food.

"Do you think we can get some shopping in too?" Lara pleaded with hopeful eyes.

"I suspect we can fit that in."

Beaming with excitement, Lara helped her make a list of the most important items they wanted to buy while they were in the city, and Alec chimed in with a few suggestions of his own.

"This is starting to sound like a major operation," Shannon said. "I didn't realize you needed bedspreads and clothes. We'd better leave early."

"The campus tour will take a couple of hours," Alec told her, "and if we call this afternoon, we might be able to set up meetings with our advisors."

"That's a good idea," Shannon said. "I want you to take as much time as you need to get familiar with the campus."

"Better take a book along so you'll have something to do while you're waiting for them," Deborah said soberly.

Shannon smiled. "What a lovely thought. Me, with time to sit and read while I wait for my children. Although I might want to go on the tour with you." She looked anxiously at the twins. "If you don't mind, of course. I'd like to get a look at the university too and see where your dorms are."

Alec mentioned something about checking out the sports facilities, and Shannon let their banter sweep over her, enjoying the normalcy of it all. A year ago, she'd never have dreamed she would transplant herself and her children from Scotland to Oregon, and the fact that they lived in such luxurious surroundings as the Paisley mansion over-whelmed her when she stopped to think about it. They were truly blessed.

Lara touched her arm. "Mum?"

"Sorry—what did you say?"

"Running shoes. Alec needs a new pair. Put that on your list, please."

Alec helped himself to another roll. "They don't have to be fancy."

Shannon nodded and jotted it on her pad. Lara peeked over at her list. "I was wondering ..." Lara's voice trailed off, and for a moment nobody spoke.

Shannon looked up at her. "What?"

"When we go to Portland, will we finally get to meet Grandmother Beth—like you promised?"

Shannon's stomach dropped. She'd only recently met

her mother again—for the first time since she was four years old. While their relationship had started out strained, they'd worked through the awkward reuniting phase and begun to develop a strong bond. She wanted her twins to have a meaningful relationship with Beth too. However, for some reason the thought of introducing Alec and Lara to their grandmother still made Shannon a little nervous.

"I'm not sure we'll have time," she said, avoiding the twins' eager gazes. They knew that Beth Jacobs lived in the Portland area and operated her Gourmet on the Go food carts in the city. Shannon had put off introducing them to their grandmother as long as she could, but after many recent family discussions—some heated—she'd finally agreed it was time they met her. "Let's see how it goes, shall we?"

"OK." Lara turned back to her food, and Shannon was surprised at her easy acceptance.

"Let's leave really early," Alec said. "That list is getting pretty long."

"The Purls are going to meet tonight," Shannon said, referring to the Purls of Hope, her close circle of friends who met at the store to knit together for charitable causes. Shannon loved the group, but today she felt as though she already had a full plate. "I'm not sure I should go. If we're going to spend all day in Portland tomorrow ...."

"Maybe you should postpone it," Deborah said.

Shannon thought about it. "I hate to have everyone change their schedules on my account."

Deborah shook her head. "Personally, I think you should get to bed early tonight. You're already burning the candle at both ends as it is."

In the end, Shannon called her friend Joyce Buchanan, who offered to check with the group members, and all agreed to postpone the gathering. Shannon was glad, as she knew she'd have a full day with Alec and Lara the next day. The thought of taking the twins by Beth's food cart weighed heavily on her mind, but she'd finally decided it would be a good thing. Better to do it now than to put it off and cause their family more tension over it.

Back at the store, she talked to her employees and learned that Melanie had already committed to work at The Flower Pot the next day. Carrie Weston, however, happily accepted the offer of a full day's work at the store with Essie. To Shannon's surprise, Essie suggested that Shannon borrow her car.

"I'm not insulting your truck or anything—I think it's cool," she insisted. "But driving into the city and all ... and the kids will want to make a good impression on campus."

"Are you worried that their advisors will think we're hillbillies or something?" Shannon teased.

Essie laughed. "Since you put it that way—yes. Take my car. It's easy to drive."

With a chuckle, Shannon reluctantly agreed.

*　　*　　*

After a successful trip to Portland University and a cheerful visit with Beth, Alec drove them home late the next afternoon. They swung by the Paisley Craft Market to swap vehicles and arrived at the mansion at ten minutes past six.

Deborah met them in the foyer. "Perfect timing. Dinner's ready."

"Thank you, Deborah," Shannon said. "We'll run these packages upstairs and wash up."

"Five minutes." Deborah looked pointedly at Lara and winked.

Lara laughed. "Will do. Wait until you see my new outfit!" She scurried up the stairs with her arms full of shopping bags. Alec followed, balancing several parcels on his carton of textbooks.

"Oh, Shannon," Deborah said. "A man came to the door this morning, asking for you."

Little needles prickled the back of Shannon's neck. "Did he leave his name?"

"No—and I asked. I'd never seen him before."

Shannon forced an easy smile. "Probably a salesperson."

Deborah shrugged. "I suppose. But they're usually more than happy to leave their name and contact information— and a stack of pamphlets selling whatever widget they're peddling." She turned away and headed toward the kitchen.

Shannon strode to the key pad by the front door to double-check that the alarm was set. Once satisfied, she hugged her arms around her body, trying to fight the chill creeping over her.

Fredo's dead. Why do I still feel like someone's stalking me?

9

Paisley Craft Market & Artist Lofts stayed busy all morning the next day. Shannon zipped between her office, the check-out, the coffee shop, and the sales floor without a break.

A pastels class met in the coffee shop at ten o'clock, and when the class let out, several of the students remained in the store to browse the art supplies. Essie watched the counter while they shopped, and Shannon helped locate items for the students. In the whirl of activity, Shannon almost missed the young woman in capris and a striped tank top climbing the stairway to the lofts. She wasn't one of the tenants, but she looked slightly familiar. *Something about her demeanor seems odd …*

"Excuse me," Shannon said to the art student she'd helped find a pad of watercolor paper. She strode to the stairway and followed the young woman up.

Standing at the top of the stairs, Shannon could see the doors to all the lofts. Two of them were open, indicating that those artists were in the store and probably working in their small studios. But the young woman she'd followed stood before Fredo Benson's closed door, with her hand on the knob.

Shannon stepped forward. "May I help you?"

The young woman yanked her hand off the knob and whirled. Her short, curly hair bounced off her tanned face, eyes wide with surprise. "Hi. Is—uh—I'm looking for Fredo."

"Are you a friend of his?"

"Um, I took a class from him, and I thought I left something in his loft. Will he be in today?"

She hasn't heard the bad news yet. Shannon softened her tone. "I'm sorry to have to tell you, but Fredo passed away."

The girl looked down at the floor. "Oh. I see."

"I thought we'd contacted all of his students, but I guess we missed you. Were you here Friday for his painting class?"

"No, I was in his session last Tuesday."

Shannon nodded. "It happened over the weekend. There was some information about it in the newspaper, and an obituary."

"I didn't see it," the girl said quickly.

"I'm sorry you had to find out this way. I can't let you into his loft, but if you'd like to leave your name and phone number and tell me what item you think you left, we'll contact you if we find it."

The girl glanced sideways at Fredo's shut door, then the stairway. "I could just stop back in a few days."

Shannon shrugged, feigning disinterest, but she was determined to get the girl's name and pass it on to Chief Grayson. "It would make it simpler if you left your contact information—might save you a trip if we don't find it."

"OK. I'm Chloe Kitchener." She rattled off her phone number, and Shannon whipped her cellphone out of her pocket and entered it. "And what was it that you left behind at the class?"

"A brush case."

Shannon stood between Chloe and the stairway. The young woman kept glancing toward it as though ready to bolt.

"I'll look for it as soon as the police give me permission." She'd expected Chloe to express surprise that the police were involved, but the girl didn't bat an eyelash. "What does your case look like?"

"Oh, brown leather. And it has brushes in it. Four, I think. Or maybe six. Nice ones. I don't want to lose them."

"Of course." Shannon smiled and put her phone away. "I'll let you know right away if we find it, Chloe."

"OK." She stirred as if ready to leave.

Shannon stood aside. "You know, our store manager, Essie Engleman, is offering a class in acrylics now, if you're interested."

"No thanks. I was just hoping to find my case." Chloe hurried past her and scrambled down the stairs.

Shannon followed, watching as Chloe practically ran across the store and out the front door.

Essie paused in her work and stared after the girl. "Who was that?" she asked as Shannon reached the bottom of the stairs.

"Chloe Kitchener. She claims to be one of Fredo's students. Have you ever seen her before?"

"Yeah, maybe." Essie frowned. "She wasn't here for the class on Friday."

"No, she says she took an earlier class with him, and she'd left something behind. She wanted inside Fredo's loft. I think I'll give the chief a call and let him know about it."

"Good idea," Essie said. She turned to greet a woman approaching the counter with her arms full of art supplies.

Shannon retreated to her office and opened her address book for Chief Grayson's non-emergency number. Before she could place the call, the desk phone rang.

"Paisley Craft Market, Shannon speaking."

"Hello," said a man whose voice she didn't recognize. "I understand you rent space to artists and offer facilities for classes?"

"Yes, we do." Shannon sat down at her desk and quickly accessed the computer file with her chart of the current rentals. A glance confirmed what she'd already known. All twelve of the lofts were currently rented, if she counted Essie and Fredo. "I'm afraid we don't have an opening at the moment. We should have one soon, though. What sort of media do you work in?"

"I paint and do collage and small sculpture." His voice had a clipped accent, which Shannon thought might be Asian. "May I come and look at your facility?"

"You might want to wait a week or two. I'm fairly sure we'll have an opening by then. If you'd like to come by sooner to check out the store and a typical artist's loft, we could show you that, as well as the resources we offer."

"Hmm, yes. I'm in Forest Grove," he said. "I'll wait to come by until you have a loft space free. You say it will be soon?"

"Should be. Would you like to leave your name and number?" Shannon poised a pen over her memo pad. "I'll call you once it's available."

"No. I will call back," he said, then hung up.

Shannon took the telephone receiver from her ear and stared at it. His evasiveness seemed odd to her. Although she hadn't managed to get his name, his phone number was stored in her caller ID, and she copied it on her memo pad.

"Shannon?"

She swiveled her chair to face the door. Essie stood in the doorway, looking slightly frazzled. A pen stuck out from behind one ear, and she held a pricing gun in her hand.

"One of Fredo's students is out front, and he claims he paid for classes in advance. He's demanding a refund."

"Oh boy." Shannon stood. "I'll go talk to him."

A young man who looked to be in his early twenties stood near the checkout with his hands shoved in the pockets of his ragged jeans, a sullen expression on his face.

"Hello," Shannon said with a smile. "I'm the store owner. I understand you've asked for a refund?"

"Yeah." His hard gaze challenged her. "I paid for six sessions with Fredo, and I only got two. I'm sorry he's dead and all that, but it would really help to get the forty bucks back."

"I see. Here's the deal: Our artists collect their class fees themselves, and at the moment, I don't have access to Fredo's records."

"Because the police took them?"

"That's right." Obviously this young man had read the papers. "As soon as I'm able, I'll look into this for you. I don't think it will be more than a few days—a couple of weeks at most. Let me take your name and phone number."

The student wasn't happy, but he complied.

"I'm sorry you got caught in all this," she said. "I'll call you soon."

He was still scowling when he left, and though the sum was a small one, Shannon wondered how badly he needed it. She sighed and thought about all the little business headaches she'd had since Fredo's death and decided to write them down and mention them to Chief Grayson. Each incident by itself seemed fairly innocuous, but overall, Fredo's sudden absence was causing more disarray in the store's operations than it should.

Shannon joined Essie at the counter as the assistant manager finished cashing out a customer.

"A Mrs. Reid just called for you. I told her you'd call her back," Essie said.

Shannon slapped her palm to her forehead. "The bag! Things have been so hectic lately, I keep pushing it off."

"Is that the antique bag you're replacing the beads on?"

Shannon nodded. "And I've got it at my home, so I can't do any work on it while I'm here today. I'll call her. I hope she's in an understanding mood."

As soon as Carrie arrived for her shift, Shannon returned to her office and called Mrs. Reid. Fortunately, her client was not upset with the delay. Shannon hung up and leaned back in her chair, thinking about the day's events.

A moment later, she picked up the phone and called the police station.

"Hello, Shannon," Chief Grayson said. "What's going on at the craft market today?"

Shannon couldn't believe her ears. *He almost sounds happy to hear from me.* "Nothing major, but I've had a few small incidents I wanted to run by you."

"Let me hear them. I'd rather have too much information than too little."

She started in with the nameless caller who had inquired about a loft. "It was probably nothing. We get those calls fairly often. But it seemed odd because he didn't want to leave his name and number. I got his number from the caller ID though."

"What else?" Grayson asked.

She went on to describe her interaction with Chloe Kitchener and the student who'd asked for a refund. "I have no way of telling whether or not any of these students has an ulterior motive for what they ask. I thought maybe you could give me some perspective."

"You're right not to let anyone into Fredo's loft yet," Grayson said, "and you did absolutely the right thing with that girl, telling her you would look for her property. It's possible some people might use Fredo's death and the confusion surrounding it to take advantage of you."

"That's what I thought. I don't want to seem paranoid about this, but if I trust everyone blindly, somebody could really deal me a blow."

Grayson grunted in agreement. "I know we've been a little slow about releasing Fredo's loft. That's because the murder took place in his apartment, not over there at the store, and we've been busy on that front. The murder is our most important priority right now. But I haven't forgotten about the break-in you had, and I haven't ruled out the possibility of there being a connection. I want my people to go over that loft thoroughly before it's disturbed. Tell you what ..." He paused for a moment, then continued, "I'll see if we can get over there first thing in the morning."

"That would be wonderful. Thank you."

"You're welcome," he said. "And if anything else odd pops up—especially anything to do with Fredo—you let me know."

His words had jogged her memory, and Shannon sat up straight in her chair. "There *was* one other thing."

"Yes?"

"It happened yesterday, while I was in Portland with the kids. Deborah said a man came to the house, asking for me. She didn't recognize him, and he didn't leave his name."

"I'll give Deborah a call and see if we can get a lead on that guy."

Shannon smiled, relieved. "Thanks, Chief." *It's so nice when Grayson and I aren't at odds. Who knew working with him on a case could be so ... pleasant?*

— 10 —

Two police officers arrived at the store early the next day. Shannon took them up to Fredo's loft, unlocked the door, and left them to do their work.

The store and the coffee shop stayed busy all morning. Several customers asked questions about Fredo's murder. The local newspaper had run brief updates daily on the police activity on the case, and Apple Grove residents seemed to find it fascinating.

"Mrs. McClain?"

Shannon looked up from the counter to find Officer Doan staring at her. "Are you all finished in Fredo's loft already?" she asked.

"Not yet," he said, "but we found some papers in the drawer of Mr. Benson's worktable upstairs. Some of them appear to be lists of people enrolled in his classes and the amounts they paid him. I thought they might be helpful to you."

Shannon exhaled and reached for it. "Extremely. Thank you so much. Would you like me to make a copy for myself so you can keep the originals?"

"If you don't mind, ma'am."

She ran the three sheets through her copier and returned them to Officer Doan.

"Thanks," he said. "We're almost done up there. I expect

we'll be through in a few minutes, and I'll bring you a receipt for anything we take away with us."

After he'd left her, Shannon perched on the stool and studied Fredo's lists. Each sheet corresponded to a different class—acrylics, oils, and drawing—and contained the name and address of each student. Fredo had marked off each student's payments with check marks.

On the list of acrylics painting students, she found the name of the young man who'd requested a refund. Sure enough, he'd paid for all six sessions at the first class. To her surprise, one student had also made a twenty-dollar down payment toward the oils classes, but as far as she could tell, the others paid for each session individually.

Shannon found the sticky note she'd made the day before and called the young man's number. He answered almost immediately.

"H'llo?" He sounded a little sleepy.

"Hi. This is Shannon McClain, at Paisley Craft Market. You'll be happy to know, I found a record of your payment for the painting classes. The payment never reached me, as I have nothing to do with what the artists bring in for their classes. But as the owner of the store, I'll take the loss and refund your money."

"You will?" He sounded a bit perkier. "Thank you."

"I'll put your refund in the mail, unless you want to drop by the store for it."

"I can come in tomorrow for it."

"Terrific. We'll have the cash in an envelope with your name on it at the counter."

"Thanks again. I really do hope the police figure out

what happened to Fredo. He may have had a shady past, but I didn't hold it against him. He was a great teacher."

Shannon gripped the phone so hard her knuckles turned white. "What exactly do you mean by 'shady past'?"

"His time in prison." The man's voice wavered. "That's all I meant."

"What do you know about that?"

"Nothing," the man blurted. "I mean, I saw him one day at the beach without his shirt on, and I know a prison tattoo when I see one. He has more than a few. Look, I've got to go. I'll stop by tomorrow."

The line went dead before Shannon could unscramble her thoughts. *I must be the last person in Apple Grove to know about Fredo's unsavory past. Brilliant.*

She caught Essie's eye and headed for her office just as two policemen came down the stairs.

Officer Doan held out a folded sheet of paper to her. "Here you go. We're taking those papers I showed you and a few other things—it's all listed there. We'll contact Fredo's students to see if any of them talked to Mr. Benson the day of his death."

Shannon studied the list of items on the paper. "Thanks. When can we pack up his things?"

"Not yet, I'm afraid, but soon." Officer Doan smiled apologetically. "We'll let you know."

"OK." Shannon slipped into her office, sat down, and opened a new computer file. She hadn't typed two words when her phone rang.

"Paisley Craft Market, Shannon speaking."

"Hi, it's Betty."

Shannon smiled. Her good friend, who was the owner of The Apple Grove Inn, was just the pleasant distraction she needed. "Hello. How are things at the inn?"

"Very good, and very busy." Betty sighed. "But I'm sneaking out this evening for the Purls gathering. Are we still meeting?"

"I'm counting on it." Shannon had considered staying in for the evening. After all, she wasn't going to have many more nights with the twins before they left for university—and she needed to get working on Mrs. Reid's beaded bag. But she knew seeing her friends would psychologically center her and help her deal with all the turmoil going on in her life. "Wouldn't miss it."

"Good. I'll see you there."

As soon as they hung up, Essie poked her head in the door. "Shannon? There's a man out front. He'd like to speak to you."

Shannon sighed. "Is it a salesman?"

"I don't think so. He doesn't have a sample case. He's not bad looking—about twenty-five or thirty, I'm guessing, nice hair, good smell."

Shannon chuckled. Attractive men in Essie's age bracket didn't visit the craft market often. "Lead me to him."

When they reached the front of the store, Shannon did a quick assessment of the stranger and agreed with Essie's opinion. The young man was not only handsome, he was neatly dressed in khakis and a short-sleeved, striped button-up shirt.

He smiled and held out his business card to her. "Hi. I'm Jake Stager, from *The Oregon Tribune*."

Shannon's stomach plummeted. *A reporter.* "How may I help you, Mr. Stager?"

"I'm doing a story on Fredo Benson, the artist who was murdered last week."

"I'm sure you can get a lot more information on that topic from Chief Grayson than you can from me."

Stager smiled and ignored her comment. "Fredo had a studio here, I think?"

"Yes, we rent lofts to artists, and he was a tenant."

"Did you know him well?"

"Not really." Shannon glanced nervously over her shoulder. "It's probably best that you talk to the police chief about Fredo."

"Just came from his office," Stager said, still smiling. "He gave me an update on the investigation, but I'd like to write about Fredo's personal life."

Shannon folded her arms across her chest. "I don't know anything about his personal life."

"I talked to a couple of other people who knew him. I'm getting a mixed bag of impressions. Did you like Fredo?"

Shannon blinked, caught off guard by the question. "As I said, I didn't know him well. We had a business relationship only."

Stager leaned in toward her and lowered his voice. "I heard he cut off part of his ear to be like Vincent van Gogh."

Shannon tried not to let her dismay show in her face. "I don't know who you've been talking to, but really, I can't help you when it comes to Fredo Benson's personal life." She glanced around and saw a few customers watching them. "I'll have to ask you to leave, Mr. Stager. Your visit is disrupting my business."

"Sorry. I don't mean any harm." He paused. "I don't suppose I could see his studio?"

Shannon felt her anger at the young man start to rise. "No. The police have sealed it off, and I have instructions that no one is to enter."

"Not even a peek in the door?"

"Not even." Shannon fixed him with a hard gaze.

"OK," Stager said with a nod. "Sorry I bothered you."

As he headed for the door, a sudden thought occurred to Shannon.

"Mr. Stager?" she called after him.

He turned, eyebrows arched. "Yes?"

"Did you stop by my house the other day? My housekeeper said a man came by on Wednesday and wouldn't leave a name."

"That would be me." He offered a sheepish grin. "I hope I didn't cause any problems."

She scowled at him. "Next time—leave a card."

He left, and Shannon puffed out all the air from her lungs. At least she didn't have to worry about the mystery man who had asked for her at the house. Knowing it was a reporter and not a burglar would set Deborah's mind at ease.

*   *   *

Meeting with the Purls of Hope that evening turned out to be exactly what Shannon needed after her tumultuous week. She was finally able to relax in the coffee shop with no customers or employees vying for her attention, no murders or college plans or sticky relationships niggling at her. For the first time in what seemed like an eternity, she was able to sit and enjoy the company of friends whom she knew would sympathize and support her, even if they didn't completely understand the challenges she faced.

Kate Ellis, owner of Ultimutt Grooming, arrived carrying a plate of cookies and wearing jeans and a T-shirt picturing cats on the front with the phrase "Cats are like potato chips; you can't have just one" written below. She looked about eighteen with her long hair pulled back into a high ponytail, but in reality, Kate was a savvy businesswoman in her thirties. Joyce Buchanan brought half a dozen cupcakes from her bakery, Pink Sprinkles. Betty and Melanie also joined them. Shannon had designated a cabinet in the coffee shop for storing their charity projects, and each woman took out her basket containing her partially completed project.

Shannon laid a few skeins of yarn on one of the tables. "We got a new shipment of yarns in today. This lot's discontinued. I thought one of you might have a project you could use it on."

"Oh, that's beautiful." Joyce fingered a skein of pale green three-ply yarn. "I can see this as an infant sweater and hat."

"It's yours," Shannon said. "Any takers for the beige?"

"If it's the right weight, I could use some in my afghan," Melanie said. She took the skein, compared it with what she was working with, and tucked it into her basket with a nod. "Thank you."

"You're welcome."

After comparing the progress they'd made on their various knitted pieces, most of which were currently lap blankets for the hospital's cancer unit, Kate looked over at Shannon.

"Hey, what's the deal with that dead artist guy? If you don't want to discuss it, I'll shut up, but really, it's so weird."

"You've got that right," Shannon said. "It's been a difficult week in the store. People come in wanting to know more about it, and all I can do is refer them to the news articles and the police. Really, the reporters know about as much as I do."

"At least it didn't happen here." Betty adjusted her yarn as she turned a row on her afghan-in-progress.

"I'm very thankful for that." Shannon tried to concentrate on her lap robe and not think about how Melanie's ex-husband's body had been found buried in the Paisley Craft Market lawn just a few short yards from where they now sat. "I didn't know Fredo well. He'd only been a tenant here for a short while."

"Did he work in his loft often?" Betty asked.

"Yes, and I didn't have any trouble with him, aside from his prima donna attitude—which he gave to everybody. The whole situation is bizarre. The police are still investigating—they haven't let me clear out his space yet."

"That must be awkward," Joyce said. Even for a casual meeting of the Purls, she wore flawless makeup, her signature fuchsia lipstick setting off her platinum blond hair.

Joyce would show up looking smart for a car wash. Shannon looked down at her own attire with a grimace. She still wore the same rumpled outfit she'd worn all day at the store, complete with chalk residue and an unfortunate glob of glue.

Shannon leaned in toward the group. "Actually, one of the strangest things to come out of all of it is Grayson's attitude toward me."

"You mean he's got something besides 'hostile'?" Kate asked.

Joyce snickered. "Sure he does. It's called 'grumpy.'"

"Now girls." Betty peered at them over her needles. "The man isn't here to defend himself. Let's not run him into the ground."

"On that note," Shannon said, "I can honestly say he's been *nice* to me."

Joyce blinked.

Melanie's jaw dropped.

Kate burst out laughing. "Good one, Shannon."

Shannon didn't laugh. "I swear it's true. Not only has he been nice, he's been thoughtful, helpful, *forthcoming* with information about the case—information I don't even ask for. I told him early on I didn't want to get involved in his investigation. Yet he continues to confide in me about new leads, new evidence, and his opinions about it all. It's shocking, really. If I didn't know better, I'd think he'd suffered some kind of mini-stroke."

No one spoke for a few moments, and clicking needles filled the silence.

"Hmm." Joyce pursed her lips. "That explains it."

"What explains it?" Shannon asked.

"Why he's being so nice to you. He no longer views you as a threat."

Shannon scoffed. "That's ridiculous. I was never a threat."

"You were," Melanie said.

Joyce nodded her head in agreement. "You've got a gift for solving mysteries, Shannon. A natural investigative intuition. Now that you've basically told Grayson you're not going to show him up—"

"Like you've done on his last few cases," Kate interjected.

"He's being nice. Trying to keep you from changing your mind, no doubt."

"Mystery solved. Hey, maybe *I* should look into being an investigator." Joyce teased.

Shannon thought about Joyce's theory, then shook her head. "I honestly don't know what to think about Grayson."

"Why don't you want to help solve the case?" Betty asked Shannon. "The girls are right, you've got a gift. And it *does* involve your store and your former artist."

"My kids," she replied simply. "I don't want to invite any more trouble in our direction while they're living under my roof."

The women all murmured sentiments of understanding.

Shannon took out a tissue-wrapped bundle she'd brought with her. "I hope nobody minds if I do some beading tonight."

"What are you working on?" Joyce leaned over to watch as she unwrapped the package.

"It's an antique beaded bag. I'm repairing it for a customer."

Joyce gasped as Shannon revealed the glittering Art Deco purse. "That's gorgeous!"

"Oh, I love it!" Melanie exclaimed.

"It is beautiful," Shannon agreed. She turned it slowly, watching the light glint off the Italian glass beads. "I had to order vintage beads so they'd match the originals. It's a privilege to work on something this exquisite."

Kate came over to get a better look. "It's really cool, but I can't imagine taking that to the grocery store."

Shannon chuckled. "I don't think my client intends to do that. Maybe to a swanky party. Anyway, I wanted to start working on it earlier, but I haven't had a chance."

"I imagine all that's been going on has been hard on your business," Betty said.

Shannon took out her magnifying readers and examined the broken stitching on the bag. "A few of the artists commented this morning on the police being in Fredo's loft, but mostly I think they're relieved that it's being looked into."

"They'll probably be glad when you get a new tenant in," Melanie said. "They won't have to remember Fredo every time they pass his empty loft."

"And *I'll* be glad when we can get rid of that yellow police tape across the door," Shannon admitted. "The whole thing has made me rethink the way we register students for art classes."

"How's that?" Betty asked.

"I had a glitch with a student who'd paid ahead for Fredo's painting classes. I refunded his money and took the loss. And there's also a girl who insists she left something in Fredo's loft, but I can't go in yet to look for it—not until the police are finished investigating."

Joyce frowned and glanced out of the coffee shop toward the stairs leading to the artist lofts. "Why would they block off his loft? He didn't die here." She lowered her voice. "Did he?"

"Well ..." Shannon glanced around at the circle of extraordinary women and knew she could be open with them in a way that she couldn't with anyone else. Other than her best friend, Coleen Douglas, who was thousands of miles away in Scotland, these women were her closest friends. "We had a break-in here last weekend. The police think it might somehow be connected with Fredo's death, but they're not certain. They don't want his things disturbed until they're sure everything in there is checked out. The police were here today, and I expect they'll release the space soon."

Melanie and Betty nodded with sympathy, but it was clear by Kate and Joyce's shocked expressions that they hadn't heard about the break-in.

"I'm so sorry." Joyce patted her on the arm. "That must have been awful for you—and then him being murdered and all. They did say 'homicide' in the paper, didn't they?"

"I'm afraid so," Shannon said.

Kate smiled at her with sympathy. "All this chaos with the students must be hard too."

"Things have calmed down." Shannon slipped a sparkly bead over her threaded needle. "There's that one girl, though, Chloe. She's the one who claims she left her brush case in Fredo's loft, and she's called twice to see if I've found it."

"Not Chloe Kitchener?" Joyce asked.

"Yes." Shannon looked up. "Do you know her?"

Joyce shrugged. "Not well. She went to school with my Kelly."

"What's she like?"

"I don't know, nowadays. But when they were in high school, I think Chloe was considered a little wild. She hung with the wrong crowd—kids who got in trouble a lot."

"Hmm." Shannon reached for her scissors. "She's been taking art classes here, and to my knowledge, there hasn't been a problem."

"Likely she's matured," Joyce said.

"There's more," Shannon said and took a deep breath. "I found some strange sketches and a painting in Fredo's loft—of *my house*. He'd been inside, and none of us knew it."

Melanie paled. "That's terrible!"

"When did it happen?" Kate asked.

Shannon told them all about it.

"And you're really not going to do anything about this?" Betty demanded.

Shannon blinked, surprised by her friend's unusually gruff tone. "Me? No. Like I said, I'm letting the police handle it."

Melanie eyed her skeptically. "I understand why you don't want to get involved, but this just doesn't sound like you."

Shannon sighed. "You're right. It hasn't been easy for me to step aside. But ever since Alec found Fredo's body, my goal has been to keep things low-key. I don't want the kids to worry too much—especially Lara."

"I should say so, after what happened with Alton Percy," Joyce said, her mouth set in a grim line.

"So you're really going to stay out of it?" Kate shook her head. "Incredible."

Shannon tried not to resent her friend's tone. "I'm turning over a new leaf—get along with Grayson, let him do the investigating. He's an experienced professional, and I know he works very hard to uphold the law in this town."

She decided it was time to put Fredo and all the upheaval surrounding his death out of her mind. Worrying about Fredo's creepy sketches or who'd killed the eccentric artist was *not* her job. Neither was fretting over who'd tried

to steal her safe, or even the whereabouts of Chloe Kitchener's brush case. *Not tonight, anyway.*

She smiled brightly at her friends. "I think the coffee's
done, and Kate and Joyce brought refreshments that look
absolutely scrumptious. Are we ready for a break?"

— 11 —

"**Y**ou can pack up Fredo's things anytime now," Grayson told Shannon on Monday morning. "I've been in touch with his family."

"How are they doing?" Shannon asked.

Grayson sighed. "It's hard for them. The medical examiner hasn't released the body yet. Maybe cleaning out his apartment and the loft will give them something else to think about this week." He handed Shannon a piece of paper. "Here's his father's cellphone number, if you want to talk to him and arrange a time for them to come."

"Should I let them pack his stuff?"

"It makes no difference as far as we're concerned." Grayson ran a hand through his sparse hair. "If you don't want them poking around, go ahead and box Fredo's things up. On the other hand, if you're busy and it's too much trouble …"

"I'll take a crack at it. I want to look for Chloe Kitchener's brush case." Shannon looked up at him. "I take it this means you didn't find any evidence of a crime upstairs."

"No. We don't believe any crimes were committed in the lofts. I've still got the painting that was on Fredo's easel in his loft—the one of your garden. And we've got the sketchbook and some other papers, along with his computer and phone, as evidence. I won't let go of those until we look into your store break-in further. I want to find out if Fredo had anything to do with that and what he was doing in your house, taking pictures."

"I'd like to know that too." Shannon felt a shiver run through her. "It still rankles me that I let a convicted art forger lease space here."

Grayson took out his pocket notebook and flipped the pages. "We've been contacting all of his students."

"Have you learned anything useful?"

"Two of them have records too, but neither of them was in jail at the same time and place as Fredo Benson."

"Meaning?"

He shrugged. "Meaning nothing, unfortunately. If they *had* been in jail together, that might indicate they were partners in crime once they got out."

"Am I allowed to know who they are?" Shannon asked.

"I think you should know, for your own safety. One is this Chloe Kitchener you mentioned."

"*Chloe?*" Shannon recalled what Joyce had said about her being wild in her youth.

Grayson nodded. "She's been arrested several times for shoplifting. The first time was during her high school junior year, and the most recent time was about two years ago."

"She was trying to get into Fredo's loft shortly after we found him dead!"

"I suggest you keep a close eye on her when she's in the store." Grayson's grim face told her not to take it lightly. "Based on her history, she's not above stealing from a dead man."

"Who's the other one?"

Grayson glanced at his notes. "Name's William Trevor."

"I think I know who he is. I've talked to him a few times. He seems like a nice enough fellow."

"He was busted for marijuana possession once—that was ten years ago. He very well may be clean now, and he told me he'd never met Fredo before he saw the ad for the painting class. But watch yourself."

Shannon nodded. "I will. Thanks."

She walked with Grayson to the front door. After he was gone, she suddenly felt vulnerable, but she told herself that was silly. She was no less safe than she had been before she knew the two art students had arrest records. At any given time, there might be two or three convicted felons in the building without her having an inkling of it. She couldn't live life suspecting everyone of a crime. But it would make sense to be a bit stricter in her background checks on prospective tenants.

She strode to the storage room to get a few empty cartons for Fredo's belongings, thankful that she hadn't let Chloe loose in his loft. *The girl might have left with more than a brush case.*

* * *

Shannon opened Fredo's loft door while Melanie wadded up the yellow police tape. It felt odd going into the space, knowing Fredo was dead. The empty easel still stood by the worktable. Some items had been moved about, but the police had been respectful of the dead man's belongings, and the room looked fairly neat—or as neat as Fredo had left it.

Shannon dragged in boxes, bubble wrap, and old newspapers. Then she and Melanie spent a couple of hours packing up Fredo's artworks and supplies.

Meticulously, they packed twenty-five paintings and framed or mounted drawings for transport.

"Who knew packing up one tiny little loft could be so exhausting?" Melanie asked, handing her a leather brush case. "That should fit in the box behind you."

Shannon studied it. "I wonder if this is Chloe's?" She'd previously packed a zippered, black nylon case containing a dozen watercolor brushes, but Chloe had specified leather. She unsnapped it. "Hmm, these might be Fredo's brushes." She leaned closer and squinted at the metal bands that crimped the bristles at the ends of the handles, but no telltale smears of paint remained. The owner had taken good care of them. "Guess I should give Chloe a call to be sure they aren't hers."

"I can finish boxing up this stuff." Melanie waved at the remaining blank canvases and cans of paint thinner.

"OK, but be sure to put each can of liquid in a separate plastic bag."

Melanie chuckled and reached for the box of zippered storage bags. "If anyone ever has to pack up my stuff for me, I hope it's you."

Shannon smiled. "Sorry. I'm not always so compulsive, but Fredo's father is coming to get this on Wednesday, and I'd like to make it as painless for him as possible."

She left Melanie working and stepped out into the hall. Two of the other artists' doors were open, and she could hear the pottery wheel whirring in one and snatches of conversation about sculpting coming from the other as she walked past. Downstairs, Essie had a few customers, and a man and woman sat visiting in the coffee shop. Shannon went straight to her office and called Chloe.

"Oh, wow, you found it?" Chloe sounded a little breathless and excited.

"Well, I did find a brush case—two, actually, but one wasn't leather. I'm not sure the other one is yours either. Can you describe it in more detail for me?"

"Sure—uh—well, it's leather, like I said. Brown leather."

"Is your name on it?"

Chloe hesitated. "Mm, no."

"How does it close?"

"With a snap."

"Any designs or other details that would give us a positive ID?"

"I don't think so. Why don't I just come over and look at it? I'm sure I could tell right away if it's mine."

Not so fast. Shannon wasn't about to let go of the case without proof of ownership. Good artists' brushes weren't cheap, and these looked top of the line. She opened the case again. On the fabric lining, in the corner near a loop that held one of the brush handles in place, she spotted a small inked design. After puzzling over it for a few seconds, she realized it formed a stylized monogram—FB. "OK, Chloe, I see a mark inside the case. I'm afraid this isn't the one you're looking for."

"What kind of mark?" Chloe asked.

Shannon almost laughed. "You tell me."

"Uh, there might be a … a logo. For the manufacturer, you know."

"No, this is hand drawn."

"A doodle?"

"Not exactly. I'm sorry, but I'm pretty sure now that this case belonged to Fredo. I'll put it with the rest of the things we're returning to his family."

Chloe sighed. "It *could* be mine."

"No, I don't think so. But if we find another brown leather case, I'll let you know."

Shannon hung up and flopped back in her chair, mentally exhausted. Chloe had tried hard, but she wasn't getting a souvenir from Fredo's loft.

Stealing from a dead man—some people will do anything.

Shannon picked up the case and headed out to the sales area just as Melanie came down the stairs. They both joined Essie at the checkout counter.

"Well?" Melanie asked.

"Nope. Not Chloe's." Shannon opened the brush case and showed them the inked design. "I think those are Fredo's initials. She had no clue."

Essie shook her head. "Unbelievable. Sounds like she described Fredo's case as well as she could and hoped you'd give it to her."

"Looks that way." Shannon closed it and handed it to Melanie. "Would you mind putting it in with that last batch of his stuff?"

"Not at all." Melanie took it from her. "Want me to lock up Fredo's loft?"

"Yes. I don't want anyone going in there until his folks come for his stuff." Shannon took the key from her pocket and gave it to Melanie.

Essie twisted a lock of her long hair around one finger. "You know," she said, leaning in and lowering her voice, "I sort of thought Chloe had a crush on Fredo. Do you think there could've been bad blood between them because he didn't return the feeling?"

Shannon raised her brows. "It's an interesting theory."

To Shannon, Chloe seemed a little old for a schoolgirl-type infatuation, but it might explain why she wanted something of Fredo Benson's so badly. On the other hand, since the girl had a record of thefts, Shannon had to wonder if Chloe simply wanted to capitalize on owning a piece of memorabilia that had belonged to the dead artist. *There's no doubt that Chloe's a thief. Is she a murderer too?*

* * *

Tuesday evening, Lara and Alec started packing for school.

I will not cry. I will not cry. Shannon repeated the mantra in her mind as she watched her twins empty their shelves. *I will, however, find something else to do that doesn't involve consuming a thousand pity calories in one sitting.*

Deborah offered to help the twins with their laundry, and Shannon decided it was long since time she worked some more on Mrs. Reid's antique beaded bag. She hadn't put a single stitch into the bag since the Purls' gathering, and she'd promised to have it finished by the end of the month.

"Are you sure you don't need me?" Shannon stood in the doorway of the laundry room. "If not, I probably should put in an hour or two on a restoration project."

"Go ahead, Mum," Alec said.

"We'll be fine," Deborah added as she smeared stain remover on one of Lara's shirts.

Confident the twins were in capable hands, Shannon climbed the grand staircase to her bedroom and took the Art Deco handbag from a drawer in her highboy dresser. She loved the beaded bag, which was probably made in the 1920s. It was larger than most handbags of that period, and it bore a beautiful, stylized floral pattern made with Italian glass beads. Unfortunately, the stitching had broken in several places, and quite a few beads were missing. Shannon needed to use her keenest skills to replace them with vintage beads she'd special-ordered.

The study next to the drawing room, where Victoria had installed a worktable, seemed the most logical spot to set up her project. Shannon gathered the supplies she would need and carried them and the bag downstairs. She loved the study, with its floor-to-ceiling bookshelves on two walls. Victoria had managed to keep a light, airy feeling in the room with lemon paint and curtains and cushions made from pastel fabrics.

She sat at the well-stocked table near one of the windows. Late-afternoon sunlight streamed in, illuminating the bag. She gazed at it for a minute. Just holding it in her hands gave her pleasure, and seeing the glass beads glint in the light sent a thrill through her. Using her extensive training, she would be able to restore the piece to the way it had looked ninety years ago. She intended to do such a good job that only experts would be able to tell it had been repaired.

Her first task was to tighten several strands of loose

stitches. In order to do that and replace the missing beads, she needed to open the lining's seam on one side and work between it and the outer fabric. That way, her stitches wouldn't show inside the bag. With painstaking care, she began to clip the tiny stitches of silk thread that held the fabric layers together. *Opening the seam three or four inches should be enough.*

As she worked, she reflected on how Mrs. Reid was fortunate to own such an exquisite and rare piece. Its size, pattern, and the types and variety of beads used placed its value in the thousands of dollars, Shannon was sure.

She sucked in a breath and raised her chin as a new thought struck her. *Did Fredo Benson break into my home because he wanted this bag?*

She recalled what Grayson had told her about the time stamps on Fredo's photographs. He'd broken into the Paisley mansion less than a week before he died. The bag was in her possession then. *Why didn't he find it in my drawer?* Was it possible he wasn't there to steal—only to look and take pictures for his art? If he'd merely wanted inspiration, he could have simply asked to come and view her home. She would have let him see the gardens and the sculptures and paintings in the foyer, at least. Fredo didn't need to sneak around or enter her house without permission.

A new idea hit her. When she had first received the Art Deco bag, she'd put it in the safe at the store. A few days later, she'd brought it home to work on. After her first session with the bag, she hadn't left it in the study. She'd hidden it away in her grandmother's old hiding place—beneath a loose tile in the east turret. At the time, she'd lamented the fact that Victoria hadn't installed a safe in the mansion. That would have been much easier to access than that cache in the dusty old tower room that her mother had used as a darkroom. About a week later, she'd taken the bag out to work on it again, and after that, she'd decided it was too much trouble to take it back to the turret room. With the first-class security system Michael's friend had installed for her, she thought it would be safe enough in her dresser—provided everyone in the house could remember to turn on the alarm.

Either Fredo wasn't looking for the bag when he broke into my house, or he'd come looking for it here while it was in the store's safe. Or perhaps he sneaked in the house during the brief time I had it hidden away in the turret.

At any rate, if he *had been* looking for the bag, he hadn't found it.

It was definitely something to discuss with Chief Grayson—later. For the moment, she needed to concentrate on the bag.

A few strands still hung loose, and Shannon drew them tighter, so that all of the original beads lay snugly against the backing fabric. She stitched the threads firmly in place. Then she opened the vials of Italian beads and held a few against the material. She compared other parts of the design with the damaged portion and selected a series of six beads to add. To her satisfaction, the match with the original beads was so good she couldn't tell the difference. Buying vintage beads took quite a bit of cash, but Mrs. Reid had agreed that replacing them with less expensive materials wouldn't do at all. Look-alikes seldom truly looked like the original under close examination.

Shannon threaded her long needle, which was so thin the silk thread barely fit through the eye. She stacked the six beads along the shaft and put her left hand inside the bag. As she opened the clipped seam with her fingers, she felt something hard and paused. She'd noticed a lump before, but assumed it was just a thick place in the seam where several pieces of fabric came together.

But now she felt something else—a solid, irregular object.

After carefully laying down the needle so that her beads didn't slide off, she gently opened the bag and examined the lining. The silk fabric was anchored in several spots to the seams of the outer material, so she couldn't turn the lining inside out. She opened a drawer on the front of the table, took out a magnifying glass, and turned on the brass table lamp.

The last thing she wanted to do was to further damage the bag. Holding it close to the lamp, she could see something glint through the seam. She probed gently along it, her excitement growing. She used the magnifying glass to examine it again.

A *small piece of jewelry.*

Further scrutiny convinced her it was the head of a jeweled stickpin. The long shaft of the pin lay along the bottom seam, stuck between the stitches. It was a wonder she hadn't found it earlier, although the thickness of the outer material of the bag did cause substantial ridges of fabric along the seams. She grasped the head of the pin and very slowly worked it until it slid out and she could remove it from the bag.

Her heart raced as she gazed down at the lovely item in her hand. *The pin must be very old, and if the stones in the butterfly design are genuine rubies and diamonds, very valuable too.* She turned it over and examined it closely with her magnifying glass. On the back of the butterfly she found an "18k" notation stamped into the gold and a small symbol she couldn't identify—perhaps a mark used by the jeweler who'd crafted the pin.

Shannon sat back and exhaled. This was certainly a matter to inform her client about. She looked at her watch. The sun had set, and it was now past eight-thirty. She decided to wait until morning to call Mrs. Reid and ask if she knew about the pin. In light of recent happenings, Shannon didn't want to keep the valuable item any longer than necessary, and she'd be relieved when it was back in the owner's hands.

Studying the pin, she realized one odd thing about it was that it came out of the bag without an end cap. *There must have been one on its sharp end, or it would have worked its way through the material at some point.* She put her fingers inside the lining and carefully felt every bit of the seam where the pin had rested. About three inches beyond where she'd found the jeweled head, a little bump met her fingertips. She smiled. The cap must have caught on the fabric and remained in the seam when she pulled out the pin. Now if she could just work it out along the same path without having to take out more of the seam ...

Nearly fifteen minutes later, her gentle, patient labor was rewarded, and she managed to extract the tiny cap. She pushed the end of the golden pin's shaft into it and admired the completed piece, marveling at its exquisite workmanship.

Who hid this pin in the lining of the bag? And why?

— 12 —

A strident beeping yanked Shannon from her slumber. The security alarm seemed to scream from all directions. She hated the sound of it; the incessant blare made her pulse race and her head pound.

She fumbled with her bedside lamp and looked at the clock. *Quarter past two.* Clad in her *Oor Wullie* pajamas, she ran out into the hall, flipped on the light, and squinted at the keypad. The small screen displayed codes for the various sensors in the system, and she read "46." *What is that?* Not the front or back doors. She punched in the digits to reset the alarm, and suddenly blissful silence surrounded her. She ran a finger down the list taped to the wall beside the keypad until she came to number forty-six. *A window sensor on the first floor.*

The phone in the bedroom began to ring, and she dashed back in to answer it.

"McClain residence."

As she'd expected, the caller was with the security company, and he asked the now-familiar question: "Would you like me to call the police?"

"Yes, thank you." Shannon hung up.

"Mum?" Lara stood in the doorway in her pajamas, rubbing her eyes.

Alec came up behind her and nudged her into Shannon's bedroom. "What's going on?"

Before Shannon could answer, Deborah appeared, panting, in the doorway.

"Was that the police?" she asked, squeezing into the room next to Alec.

"It was the security company. The window alarm in the study was tripped," Shannon said. "The police are on their way."

"Should we go down and take a look?" Alec's gaze darted toward the door. "It might take the police ten minutes or more to get here."

"Well—"

"I don't think you should do that." Deborah shook her head emphatically. "It could be dangerous."

Shannon turned to her. "Did you see anything suspicious on your way up here?"

"No, but once I decided I'd rather be up here with you than alone in my room, I ran and didn't look around."

Shannon made a quick decision. "You come with me, Alec. Lara, Deborah—you two stay here near the phone."

Lara gripped Shannon's arm. "Be careful, Mum." Her eyes were wide with fear, reminding Shannon of the turmoil Lara had recently experienced when Alton Percy died, and she found herself at the center of a dangerous murder investigation. Shannon never wanted to see her daughter suffer like that again.

Shannon gave her a reassuring hug. "I'll be careful. I'm sure it's nothing—probably the strong wind tripped the alarm."

Lara nodded. "I hope so."

Shannon grabbed a flashlight from the bottom shelf of her nightstand and handed it to Alec.

He switched it on and laid his hand on her arm. "Let me go first."

Before she could protest, Alec strode from the room toward the top of the stairs. She scurried to catch up and crept down the steps behind him, wishing they'd stopped long enough to grab something that could be used as a weapon.

A sliver of light spilled into the foyer from the hallway that led to the kitchen, but the other rooms below lay in darkness. They crept along with Shannon close on Alec's heels.

He shined the beam of the flashlight on the front door and foyer windows. "Nothing here."

At the doorway to the study, Shannon shivered. *A few hours ago, I was sitting in there, working on the handbag. Was someone watching me through the window?*

Alec turned and whispered, "Ready?"

She nodded, and he snaked his long arm around the doorjamb to flip the light switch in the study. Shannon peered into the room beneath his arm.

Everything looked as quiet and inviting as it had earlier. She'd left the containers of Italian beads on the worktable by the window, and they were still in place.

"Is that the window that tripped the alarm?" Alec's voice cracked.

"Yes. But everything looks fine."

"Should I close the curtains?"

Shannon shook her head. "Better not touch anything until the police get here."

"Maybe you shouldn't have shut off the alarm."

"I reset it, so it's on now." She rubbed her temples. "I merely stopped the horrific beeping."

"That thing is really obnoxious. You don't suppose it would go off if a branch touched the window, do you?"

Shannon considered it for a moment, then shook her head. "There aren't any shrubs or trees close enough to that window." She heard the faint sound of an engine. "That must be the police."

Alec headed for the front door, and Shannon trailed after him, wondering if she had time to run upstairs for her robe.

"Mum?" Lara called softly from the stair landing.

Shannon looked up at her and smiled as she switched on the lights. "It's OK, love. The window doesn't look like it's been opened. Could you fetch my robe?"

"Sure." Lara dashed off, and Shannon turned her attention to the door.

Alec opened it before the officer could ring the bell.

To Shannon's relief, one of the men she knew stood on the porch. "Officer Brownley," she said as brightly as she could manage. "We've got to stop meeting like this."

He grinned. "Everything all right here, ma'am?"

"I think so. It's just—oh, thank you." Shannon turned as Lara raced down the steps with her robe in hand. Shannon took it and hastily pulled it on. "I was working this evening in the study, and that's the window where the alarm went off a few minutes ago. It looks all right now, at least from the inside. We didn't go outside."

"We'll take a look," Officer Brownley said. "Can you show me the window, please?"

Shannon led him toward the study. Alec and Lara followed a few steps behind, and Deborah stood halfway down the staircase, watching them.

"Was the light on in here?" the officer asked as they entered the study.

"No. Alec turned it on. He and I came down together."

Officer Brownley flicked a glance at Alec, who still held his flashlight, though he'd turned it off. The officer walked over to the window and bent to peer at the windowsill and the casement.

Lara appeared in the doorway. "Another police SUV just drove up."

"That'll be the chief," Officer Brownley said.

"I'll go let him in." Shannon was surprised Chief Grayson had come out for what might turn out to be nothing but a false alarm. She hurried across the foyer, but Deborah beat her to the door.

"Hello, Miss Waters, Mrs. McClain." Grayson glanced grimly about as he entered the foyer. "I understand you've had another disturbance."

"Yes, unfortunately." Shannon told him what had happened, and he went to join Officer Brownley in the study. A minute later, they emerged, and the chief asked her the best way to get to the spot outside the study window. She took them through the kitchen and let them out the back door, waiting while the two men walked through the garden and examined the ground near the wall and the window.

When they came back inside, everyone gathered around the two policemen in the kitchen.

"It looks as though someone was out there tonight," Grayson said. "There are a couple of partial shoe prints, but I doubt they're distinctive enough to be of much help. In light of last week's happenings, I'm going to have Officer Brownley dust the outside window frame for fingerprints. We've also got another patrolman scouting for vehicles that don't belong in the immediate area, but nothing has turned up so far. Whoever was here probably hit the road long before we arrived."

Shannon nodded. "Thank you very much, Chief."

"Would you like Officer Brownley to stay here for the rest of the night?"

"Oh, that won't be necessary." Shannon looked around at her children and Deborah.

Alec stepped forward. "You don't think they'll come back, do you, Chief?"

Grayson shrugged. "I doubt it. I suspect the alarm and police presence are enough to keep them away, at least for tonight. But I *am* concerned." He turned to Shannon. "It's clear that someone has an eye on you."

Shannon frowned. "I'm beginning to suspect this is connected to the break-in at the store. What do you think?"

"It may be." Grayson jangled his keys at his side. "Reset your alarm, and we'll keep a patrolman in the neighborhood until daylight."

"That's not very far off," Deborah said.

Shannon glanced at the kitchen clock, startled to find it was nearly 3 a.m. "I'll be up in a couple of hours anyway."

"Get what sleep you can," Grayson said. "We'll talk more later."

Shannon walked him and Officer Brownley to the door.

Lara appeared at her side the moment they were gone. "Mum, that was pretty scary. I don't like the thought of you and Deborah being here alone after we leave on Monday."

Shannon pulled her into a quick embrace. "Don't worry, honey. Chief Grayson is going to find out who's behind all this. And the alarms *are* doing their job, right?"

"Yes—so far."

As if to prove her point, Shannon turned to the keypad on the wall and made sure the entire system was set once more to protect them. She bid Deborah good night and walked upstairs with the twins, keeping up a cheerful banter until they all headed for their separate rooms.

Once alone in the bedroom her grandmother had decorated with so much thought, Shannon hung up her robe and climbed into bed. She turned off the lamp and gazed at the faint stars, visible through the panes opposite, where the tall French windows opened onto her balcony. Never in her life had she dreamed she would have such a beautiful, peaceful place to slumber.

But sleep eluded Shannon. The thing she'd intended to tell Grayson about—Mrs. Reid's beaded bag—had slipped her mind. *Should I call him now?* Morning would come soon enough, she supposed. Still, she couldn't help thinking about the intruder and about Fredo being murdered in his own bedroom—in his bed. Every little creak of the house's timbers startled her anew.

With a sigh, she rolled over and drew the coverlet up over her ear, trying not to think about how much she'd like to take a bigger role in the investigation, as it seemed to be going to nowhere fast. *Not while the kids are here. Let the police handle it.*

She repeated the words in her mind many times before sleep finally took hold.

— 13 —

Shannon took the beaded bag to the store with her the next morning and put it in her office safe. A few minutes after she'd unlocked the front door and flipped the sign to "Open," a tall, dark-haired man entered the store. His gaze skimmed over the colorful display of yarns in their wall bins and trays filled with beads in various textures and hues. When he spotted the paint supplies, his mouth twitched.

Observing him from behind the counter, Shannon couldn't quell the slight anxiety that the man's presence triggered. Quickly, she slid the bills she'd been counting into the proper sections of the cash tray and closed the register drawer. "May I help you?"

"I'm Carlo Benson."

"Of course. You must be Fredo's father." Shannon saw the resemblance at once, and her anxiety defused. She stepped out from behind the counter with her hand extended. "I'm so sorry about your son."

"Thanks. I, um, came to pick up his things. Do you know where his loft is—was?" The man's voice wavered with emotion.

"Yes, I'll take you to it. We've already boxed up his things for you."

Shannon spent the next fifteen minutes helping him load Fredo's belongings into his van.

"Thank you for all your help," Mr. Benson said. "Was my son up-to-date on his account with you?"

"Yes, he was. Thanks for asking."

He nodded and looked around bleakly, as though seeking some other remembrance of his son. "It's a difficult thing. His mother and I planned to visit him after he was settled here a while. He showed such great promise. We hoped he could start a new season of his life—a pleasant, successful one."

"He was a very talented artist," Shannon said. "His work showed great passion."

Mr. Benson sighed. "If only he hadn't gotten mixed up with the wrong people. We thought—we hoped—he was on a better path, but ..."

Shannon reached out and squeezed his arm gently. "I'm so sorry you have to go through this, Mr. Benson."

He dashed away a tear. "You have children?"

"Yes."

"You understand, then. You want the best for them. You'd do anything you could to protect them."

Shannon let his words sink in. "I would."

He opened his mouth as though he would say more, but then his shoulders slumped. "Well, thank you."

"Goodbye," Shannon said as he turned away. She watched him climb into his van. He pulled out of the parking lot just as Chief Grayson's SUV pulled in.

I'm never going to get any work done today.

Shannon invited the chief into her office and told him about Mr. Benson's visit. "I admit, I'm glad that task is behind me."

"Always difficult." Grayson leaned against the wall.

"You must deal with it a lot in police work—talking to victims' families."

"More often than I'd like. Everything else going OK here today?"

"Actually, something odd has come up that I wanted to ask you about." Shannon motioned to a chair. "Would you care to have a seat?"

Grayson lowered his large frame into a chair, and Shannon opened the safe to remove Mrs. Reid's beaded bag.

She held up the antique bag for Grayson's scrutiny. "A client asked me to restore the beadwork on this piece a few weeks ago, and I've had it ever since. The bag itself is quite valuable, but things got more complicated last night. I was working on it at home when I discovered a piece of jewelry hidden inside the lining."

She opened the bag and showed Grayson the vintage stickpin and how it had been inserted into the seam.

"Clever hiding place," he said, stifling a yawn. His groggy expression told Shannon he hadn't mentally connected the dots yet.

She plunged ahead. "Of course, I'm going to inform the owner of the bag. I don't think she knew the pin was there, or she would have removed it before she handed the bag over to me. Or maybe she put it there in the past and forgot about it."

Grayson held the pin up close to examine it. "Are those real diamonds?"

"I think so, and rubies too, but a jeweler could tell us for sure."

"Well, regardless, it's very pretty." Grayson handed it back to her with a polite smile and glanced at his watch.

Shannon sighed. "The reason I'm telling you this is because last night before the attempted break-in, I'd been working on the bag in the study after supper. That's when I found this pin. I'm wondering if someone saw me through the window, working on it, and thought it was still in that room after I went to bed."

Grayson sat up straight, seeming to snap to attention. "Perhaps that's what the thief is after? It might explain all the break-ins you've experienced."

"Precisely! I can't help but wonder that myself."

He furrowed his brow. "There is one problem with that theory. I don't recall the bag being in the safe the night the store was broken into."

"No. I had it at home. But it *was* here in the store for a while, after the owner first brought it to me. It wasn't until a few weeks later that I put it in a safe place at the house because I wanted to work on it in the evenings. I didn't even think of it the night the thieves came here, or I would have told you."

"How much is the bag worth?"

"I'm guessing several thousand dollars," Shannon said. "Out of curiosity, I made some comparisons online with similar items that have sold within the past six months. A bag of this age and size, with such a beautiful pattern—those are handmade antique glass beads from Italy—could be worth up to fifteen thousand dollars in today's market. The pin I'm not so sure about. I haven't had a chance to research it. It would probably be best to ask an expert."

He nodded and scratched his chin. "Mind if I snap a few pictures?"

"No, go ahead."

She waited while he did so with his cellphone.

"OK," he said. "Keep those locked up, and let me know what happens, all right?"

"I will."

Grayson left, and Shannon secured the pin in the bag. As she started to rewrap it in tissue, she was overcome with the eerie feeling of being watched and looked up.

Chloe Kitchener stood in the doorway, eyeing the bag.

"Chloe!" Shannon hastily wrapped it with the tissue paper. "Can I help you?"

Chloe leaned against the doorframe, blocking the exit. "I was in the neighborhood, and I thought I'd drop in and see if you'd found my brush case. Has it turned up?"

"No," Shannon said firmly. "And Fredo's family has taken all of his things away. We've cleaned out the loft. Your case wasn't there."

Chloe scowled. "OK. Thanks for nothing." With a final lingering glance at the tissue-wrapped bag, she turned away with a toss of her head.

Shannon exhaled slowly. She put Mrs. Reid's bag into the safe and shut it, then hurried out to the front of the store.

Chloe was nowhere to be seen.

"Essie, did you see Chloe Kitchener in here?"

"Yeah, she walked through a second ago, but I was taking care of Mrs. Taylor." Essie paused. "Where did she come from anyway? I didn't hear her enter through the front door."

"I don't know, but she came back to my office."

Essie's eyes widened. "I'm sorry. I didn't see her come in or I would've stopped her. She must've sneaked by me."

"It's all right."
Where had Chloe come from?

* * *

A large shipment of new merchandise arrived shortly before noon, so after Shannon ran home for lunch with Deborah and the twins, she brought Alec back with her to help Essie organize the storeroom. Melanie watched the front counter while Shannon went to her office and called the woman who had commissioned her to fix the Art Deco bag.

As soon as the word "stickpin" was out of Shannon's mouth, Mrs. Reid gave a little squeal. "A stickpin? Oh, my! Dare I hope? My dear, please tell me it's a butterfly pin."

"Yes, it is." Shannon couldn't help but smile. Mrs. Reid's joy at her discovery made her glad to be the one bringing such good news.

"Rubies and diamonds on the wings, and an elongated, marquis-shaped onyx for the body?"

Shannon studied the pin and bag that lay before her on the desk. "That's it precisely."

"Oh, what a relief! We've looked and looked for that pin. I was sure it had been stolen. How could it possibly have been in the bag, and I didn't know it?"

"It was under the lining, so it wasn't obvious," Shannon said. "Would you like me to keep it in my safe until you come for the bag?"

"No, I'd like to get the pin back right away, if you don't mind."

"Not at all."

After a bit of hemming and fumbling with her calendar, Mrs. Reid decided she couldn't get to Apple Grove that day, but scheduled a time the next day when she could retrieve the jeweled pin.

"Would you like to come to my house for it, instead of the store?" Shannon asked on impulse. "That would give us some privacy."

"Thank you—that *would* be better, I think. This is so exciting—I cannot tell you how grateful I am!"

"It's no problem." Shannon gave Mrs. Reid her home address. "I'm happy it's turned out well for you. And I'll see you tomorrow morning."

*   *   *

That evening, Deborah served fried chicken and potato salad for supper, which Lara had helped cook. They'd set the table on the back patio, and Shannon found the outdoor meal refreshing. The evening breeze off the distant ocean brought a welcome respite from the mid-August heat, and they all lingered over dessert and iced tea, talking about the twins' college courses and their future plans.

About half past seven, Shannon rose and gathered her dirty dishes. "I need to put some time in on a beaded bag tonight. The owner is coming tomorrow to get a pin I found in it, and I want to have a good part of the restoration done when she sees the bag again."

"You're going to show it to her before you're finished?" Alec asked.

"I want to show her where the stickpin was hidden. She

doesn't think she put it in there, and I'm wondering if it could possibly have been accidental. The whole thing is very odd."

Shannon took the bag to her study. Before she began to work, she stood for a moment gazing out the window. *Did someone watch me last night?* She closed the curtains, though she hated to block the beautiful view, and turned on bright lights to aid in her work.

Beading was a skill Shannon had learned long ago in Scotland, and she found it both exciting and soothing. Her bold designs stretched her creativity, but she had to work carefully. Attaching every bead in precisely the right position was a process that forced her to slow down and take each stitch deliberately. The structure and regimentation of the skill balanced the artistic thrills that ran through her as she saw the design emerge, sometimes even more beautiful than she'd imagined. From time to time, she held the bag out at arm's length, simply to admire it. The luster of the antique glass beads could not be matched by modern beads. She could well imagine the purse in a museum display.

She was nearly finished with the work she'd set out to complete that evening when Lara wandered into the study.

"How's it going, Mum?"

"Pretty good. What do you think?" She held up the bag so Lara could see the design. The beads glittered and reflected a hundred points of light.

"Oh, I love it." Lara reached for it, and Shannon let her take the bag, holding it closer and examining the beadwork. "This is gorgeous. Can I have it?"

They both laughed.

"You know," Lara said, "it reminds me of something I saw ... hmm, where was it? Oh, I know! It's in my art appreciation textbook. I was browsing through it last night, and I saw something like this."

"Really? I'd like to see it."

"Sure. Hold on." Lara hurried out of the room, and Shannon leaned back in her chair and compared her handiwork to the pattern she'd made based on the portion of the design that hadn't been damaged and a couple of photographs Mrs. Reid had brought her when she'd first delivered the bag to Shannon.

Lara soon returned, carrying a huge, thick book. "OK, now, when was the Art Deco period?"

"Hmm, 1920s and '30s, I think. But I don't suppose they called it that until later."

"Really? Oh, here it is." Lara found the page she wanted. "Look at this."

On the double-page spread were several photographs illustrating the Art Deco style in architecture, painting, and jewelry. The last one was a portrait of a woman in a sleeveless dress with a plunging neckline. Close to her chest, she clutched a handbag that appeared identical to the one Shannon held in her hand.

"Och!" Shannon stared at the picture. "The resemblance is uncanny."

"Isn't it? Now that I see them close together, it's quite eerie. The beads don't look as bright and glittery in the picture—but after all, it's a photo of a painting. Do you think your customer's bag is the one in the painting?"

Shannon glanced from the picture to the bag and back.

"I wouldn't know. The bag could be one of a kind, but it sure looks the same. I wouldn't think there were very many like it. All this beading was done by hand. Is it a famous painting?"

Lara bent closer and read the caption beneath the picture, "'Portrait by R.J. Milford, 1935.' Hmm, it doesn't say who the lady in the portrait is."

"No, but that's intriguing. I'll look up the artist online." Shannon copied down the name and smiled up at Lara. "Thanks, love. Who would have thought it?"

Lara grinned as she closed the volume and hefted it. "This book cost us an arm and a leg. I'm glad it turned out to be useful."

— 14 —

Shortly after nine o'clock on Thursday morning, a large town car rolled up the drive to the Paisley mansion. Mrs. Reid, who appeared to be in her late forties, climbed out, looking cool and chic. She sashayed to the front door in high-heeled sandals, white capris, and a matching top.

"Welcome," Shannon said from where she waited on the top step. She noted Mrs. Reid's chestnut hair, makeup, and manicure were all done to perfection.

"You have a lovely home." Mrs. Reid continued to inspect the front of the house and the flower beds as she approached.

"Thank you." Shannon led Mrs. Reid through the foyer and down the hall to the study. "My housekeeper will bring us lemonade in here—or would you prefer something else?"

"Lemonade would be lovely." Mrs. Reid looked around at the bookshelves and fine old furniture, the paintings, and the tall windows. "Charming. And so near the ocean."

"Thank you. My great-grandparents built this house. Won't you have a seat?" Shannon chose a comfortable leather chair, and Mrs. Reid sat down on the sofa opposite her.

Mrs. Reid beamed at her. "I can't tell you how grateful I am that you've found the butterfly pin."

"I'm glad it turned up safe."

Deborah entered, carrying a tray of refreshments, and Shannon introduced her to Mrs. Reid. "Deborah was my grandmother's friend and employee, and she's become very dear to me since I moved to Apple Grove."

Mrs. Reid pursed her lips. "How satisfying to have good help."

Shannon cringed. She wasn't sure that quite expressed her meaning, and she hoped Deborah wasn't insulted. When she shot Deborah an apologetic glance, she found the older woman's face smooth and carefree as she set a tall glass of iced lemonade on a coaster near each of them and a plate of small shortbread cookies on the side table.

"Enjoy." Deborah gave a dramatic bow—something she never did—and Shannon felt the corners of her mouth twitch. Clearly, Deborah was playing it up on account of Mrs. Reid's comment. "Please ring if I can be of further service." Without another word, the housekeeper turned and breezed from the room.

Lara's dramatic influence knows no bounds.

"Are those homemade cookies?" Mrs. Reid asked.

"Yes. Won't you try one?" Shannon extended the Fostoria plate to her guest. "Deborah makes wonderful shortbread."

"My favorite." Mrs. Reid seemed suitably impressed and chose one of the dainty cookies. "Now then, you said you found the pin in the lining of the handbag?"

Shannon took a cookie and set the plate down. "Yes, and I don't see how it could have gotten in there the way it was, unless someone put it there deliberately. I didn't find it the first two times I handled the bag. Of course, the seams are quite thick, and the pin is slender—except for the butterfly part."

Mrs. Reid sighed. "I have my suspicions of what happened,

but of course, I have no proof. It's always difficult with family, you know, especially when it comes to bequests."

"I do know, yes." Shannon pushed away the memories of the trouble she'd had with Victoria Paisley's relatives—her own kin, she hated to admit—after her grandmother died.

"Well, it all started when my grandmother passed away two years ago," Mrs. Reid said. "She always told me she would leave me that pin. I loved it, and I knew it was worth quite a bit of money. I looked forward to the day when it would be mine, though I loved Gram dearly. My cousin was told that the Art Deco bag would go to him. He's older than me, and the bag is worth more than the pin, so she'd designated it for her eldest grandchild. It was mentioned occasionally in the family over the years. We both expected it."

Shannon nodded and sipped her lemonade.

"But when she died and the will was read ..." Mrs. Reid shook her head. "Obviously she'd changed her mind, because the bequests were not the way she'd told us they would be."

"Oh?"

"She had every right to, of course, and I can understand why she did it. You see, my cousin—Warren is his name—had thought for more than thirty years that he would get the bag. It had been appraised at around twenty thousand dollars over a decade ago." Mrs. Reid's voice turned bitter. "I'm sure he planned to sell it as soon as they laid Gram in the ground. He couldn't wait for her to die."

Shannon flinched at the woman's harsh tone. "But it went to you instead."

"Yes. And Warren was livid. You see, Gram left me the

pin *and* the bag. Warren got only a small cash bequest. A couple of days after the reading of Gram's will, he came to see me and asked me to sell him the bag. But I wouldn't. I don't ever intend to sell it. My children can make that decision after I'm gone, but I love it, and I intend to keep it."

Shannon smiled. "It's a beautiful piece. I don't know if I'd be able to part with it either."

Mrs. Reid's lips quirked. "It *is* lovely. But the pin … after Gram died, we went through her things. My mother was her executor, and she and her half-brother, Ed Tuttle, inherited the bulk of the estate. I was helping Mother pack up Gram's things in the old house. The bag was right where she'd always kept it, but we didn't find the butterfly pin. It wasn't with her other jewelry. At first I thought it must be in her safe deposit box."

"But it wasn't?" Shannon asked.

"No. When my mother got the paperwork and went to the bank to open it, the only things in the box were some documents and Gram's wedding and engagement rings from her first marriage. Those went to my oldest daughter, per the will, but we never found the stickpin."

Shannon stared at her. "So … it was in the bag the whole time? Since before your grandmother died?"

"I would say so." Mrs. Reid shrugged. "Maybe she hid it there for safekeeping. Though I don't understand why she didn't tell us—or even her attorney."

"Was the bag damaged before you received it?"

Consternation clouded Mrs. Reid's expression. "No, it most certainly was not. I've had it nearly six years now, and it was in perfect condition until this spring. That's when my cousin Warren came to see me again, demanding I sell it to him. When I refused, he tried to snatch it out of my hand. My husband came in at just the right moment to stop him. He told Warren to leave and never return. Thankfully, I haven't seen him since. But a great many of the beads were torn loose in the struggle, as you know, and we didn't find them all. We were on the patio at the time, and some were lost in the grass."

"It's all right," Shannon said. "The source I found for antique beads matched them beautifully. I'll show you." Shannon rose and went to the worktable to retrieve the beaded bag. "I left this in here this morning because I knew you were coming. I usually keep it in a more secure place."

"Oh my, you've done a lot of work." Mrs. Reid studied it as Shannon carried the bag to her.

"Yes, I've tightened all the loose beads and begun to replace the ones that were lost."

Mrs. Reid held it close and scrutinized the area where the damage was evident. "I don't think I can tell which are the original beads and which are replacements."

"Only a few are new so far." Shannon pointed them out. "I think they match beautifully."

"They surely do! I never would have known. Now … the pin?"

"It's inside." Shannon took the bag and gently unclasped it. She opened it as wide as she could so that Mrs. Reid could see where she'd clipped the threads on the seam. "I removed a few stitches in the lining so that I could sew the beads on without pulling the needle through both layers. I didn't want any stitches to show inside."

"Very nice."

"Thank you," Shannon said. "I've slid the pin back inside, as close to the way I found it as I could get it, without forcing it. I didn't put the end cap on it this time, though. That was the hardest little thing to get out—so I put it aside over here and stuck the pin in without the end to anchor it. See how cleverly hidden it is?"

"Goodness!" Mrs. Reid's eyes widened. "I think I feel the head of it ... yes, there it is. But the stick ...."

"The shaft is right inside that seam."

"It's a wonder it wasn't bent."

Shannon nodded. "Yes. I've tried to be very careful since I discovered it. Would you like me to take it out now?"

"Oh, yes. I want to see it."

Shannon took the bag and felt the jeweled end of the pin. She was able to move it easily and draw it out. The diamonds and rubies winked in the sunlight streaming through the windows. She took the end cap from the side table, slid it over the point at the end of the pin's shaft, and laid it in Mrs. Reid's hand.

Mrs. Reid gazed down at the pin and let out a big sigh. "Yes, this is it! And in perfect condition. I feared it was lost to the family forever."

"I'm so glad I was able to find it for you."

"So am I." She looked up and smiled at Shannon. "I'd often wondered if Warren had managed to lift it before the will was read, since he wasn't expecting it to go to him. The pin isn't nearly as valuable as the bag, but it is worth eight to ten thousand—at least, that was the appraisal several years ago. It was created by Cartier's top designer in the late 1940s.

See this?" She pointed to the finely carved setting. "They don't do that sort of work around the diamonds anymore. It's a top example of the technique. And Gram was told that the rubies are flawless."

Shannon gazed at the pin. "My own grandmother left me a special piece of jewelry as well, and it meant a lot to my family." She could well imagine how Mrs. Reid felt as she recalled her own search for the valuable necklace Victoria Paisley had hidden.

"It was always my favorite of all her jewelry," Mrs. Reid said. "I even asked Gram if I could wear it once—to my best friend's party. But she said no, girls shouldn't go about wearing such valuable gems. And of course she was right. I'd have been devastated if I'd lost it then." She laughed softly. "She promised I'd have it one day. I never imagined she'd leave me the bag too. She let Warren think he would have it. I suspect it was his later behavior that changed her mind."

Shannon didn't know what to say, so she carefully clasped the beaded bag.

"Well," Mrs. Reid shifted in her chair and reached for her purse, "my cousin's reputation is neither here nor there. I'll take this pin with me today, and you can let me know when you've finished with the bag. I'm very pleased with the work you've done so far."

"Thank you." Shannon looked up as Lara entered the room. "Hello, honey. What is it?"

"Betty phoned to see if we'd all take dinner with them at The Apple Grove Inn tonight. Should I tell her you'll call back?"

"Yes, please. Oh, and Lara—"

Her daughter paused, raising her eyebrows.

"After you tell her, would you mind bringing down that textbook you showed me last night? I thought Mrs. Reid might like to see the photograph."

"Sure, Mum."

Lara breezed out of the study, and Shannon returned her attention to her client.

"When my daughter returns, I'll introduce you properly. She's starting an art appreciation class next week, and she found something in her textbook I think you'll find interesting."

"Indeed?" Mrs. Reid looked suitably intrigued.

Before long, Lara returned, carrying the hefty art book under one arm.

"Mrs. Reid, this is my daughter, Lara," Shannon said. "Lara, I'd like you to meet my client, Mrs. Reid."

Lara gave the visitor a sunny smile. "You're the one who owns that chic little bag? I'm crazy about it. And look—here's the picture Mum told you about." She sat down next to Mrs. Reid on the sofa and opened the book to a place she'd marked with a sticky note.

Mrs. Reid took one side of the volume in her hands, and Lara held up the other side, like a giant hymnbook between them.

"Oh, yes, the portrait." A soft smile wreathed Mrs. Reid's face, and Shannon could imagine her as the pretty young girl who wanted to wear her grandmother's diamond-and-ruby pin.

"You recognize it?" Lara asked.

"I certainly do. That's my Grandmother Hilliard in 1935. Isn't it a marvelous picture?"

"Brilliant," Lara breathed.

Shannon leaned over to study the picture again. "Then it *is* the same bag?"

"Indeed," Mrs. Reid said. "That portrait was done soon after Gram's marriage to Edward Tuttle. Her first marriage, you see. He commissioned the artist, Milford, to paint her portrait. Milford was all the rage at the time."

"But the portrait is in a museum now?" Lara asked, her eyes wide.

The corners of Mrs. Reid's mouth turned downward. "Yes, it was sold out of the family by necessity. When Edward Tuttle died, my grandmother was only twenty-seven, and she had a young son, Edward Junior. Grandfather Tuttle's business was on the verge of bankruptcy. It was right at the end of the Depression, and things hadn't picked up sufficiently by 1940 for the company to rebound. Poor Gram didn't know how she could stay solvent and support her little boy."

"What did she do?" Lara asked.

"Why, she took hold of the business and turned it around. But it required a great infusion of cash to get started, and that meant selling the Tuttle mansion and several nice works of art—including this portrait. The business revived, and she built it up again, as great as it had been in Mr. Tuttle's day. Five years later, she remarried, to my grandfather, Charles Hilliard. She sold the business and put away her fortune for her children."

"Incredible!" Lara's green eyes fairly glowed.

Mrs. Reid smiled. "I always thought so. My mother was the product of the union with Charles Hilliard."

"It was lovely of her to leave you such a beautiful keepsake as that handbag," Shannon said.

"She was a very generous woman." Mrs. Reid's expression turned nostalgic. "My cousin Warren, Edward Junior's son, and I and our children each received smaller bequests. I've been rather pleased with mine, even though we thought the pin was lost for the last few years."

"I'm glad Mum found it for you." Lara gazed at the picture in her textbook. "Still, it's too bad you didn't get the painting."

"It wound up in a decent museum, so I guess it's all right. Many people get to enjoy it now." Mrs. Reid sipped the last of her lemonade. "I should move along. Again, Shannon, I can't thank you enough for finding this and returning it to me."

"I'm glad this part of the story turned out well." Shannon accompanied her client to the front door. "I expect to be done with the bag in a couple of weeks."

"Just give me a call," Mrs. Reid said. "And that's a very charming daughter you have."

"Thank you so much. She and her brother are the lights of my life."

Shannon stood waving until the town car rolled out of sight. She turned to find Lara hovering in the foyer.

"Nice lady," Lara said.

"Thanks for showing her your book."

"I got a kick out of it. Maybe someday I'll have *my* portrait hanging in a museum." Lara spun in a circle and then took a bow.

Shannon gave her a quick hug. "Maybe you will."

— 15 —

That weekend, Shannon snatched a free hour while the twins were at the beach to do a little research on the artist R.J. Milford. She learned the artist rose to fame during the same era as Thomas Hart Benton and Grant Wood. Like Thomas Benton, he started out as an illustrator, but moved on to other work in his later career. Milford became best known as a portrait artist and painted many members of society's upper echelon in the 1930s and '40s. The artist died in 1970, and his works now commanded sums as high as $100,000 at auction.

Shannon didn't recognize most of the portraits she found online, but she gathered that they represented politicians, millionaires, and industrialists of the time, or members of their families. She clicked through several sites, gazing at Milford's works and absorbing his style. One page included a photo of the portrait in Lara's book. "Gram" looked the same, but the painting's caption gave her name. It was painted before she married Mr. Hilliard, Shannon remembered. Her name was listed as Delphinia Tuttle.

On a memo pad, Shannon wrote the name "Delphinia." To the left, she wrote "Mr. Tuttle." To the right of Delphinia's name, she wrote "Mr. Hilliard." She drew a line down from each of the two unions. On the Tuttle side, she wrote "grandson Warren." On the Hilliard side, she wrote "granddaughter Lois (Reid)."

Would Warren's last name be Tuttle? Mrs. Reid had said that Mr. Tuttle's son was Edward Junior, and she hadn't mentioned any sisters, or any cousins besides Warren.

In her computer search engine's window, Shannon typed "Warren Tuttle" and "Oregon." A moment later, a list of several mentions popped up. One looked like a news clipping from the previous year, and she clicked on the link.

"Aha," she said softly.

Warren had been recently arrested, according to the Portland daily newspaper. He'd been involved in a fight at his workplace and charged with assault.

This couldn't be the incident that prompted Gram's change of mind about leaving Warren a valuable bequest. Mrs. Reid said she'd had the bag for six years—since her grandmother died. Shannon speculated the workplace assault wasn't Warren's first offense and that his earlier indiscretions had led to the changes in the will.

Lara sauntered in, wearing a mint green terry wrap over her swimsuit. Her wet hair looked very dark in contrast to her smooth, pale complexion.

"Mum, the water was great. You should've come."

"Hmm," Shannon said absently.

"What are you looking at?" Lara came to stand behind her and peered over her shoulder.

"I was reading about the artist R.J. Milford, and then I thought I'd do a little browsing about the Tuttle family."

"Mrs. Reid's lot?"

"That's right."

Lara leaned closer. "Looks like her cousin Warren is the black sheep of the family, dangerous even."

Shannon looked at Lara—her dear daughter who'd had more than enough trauma for one summer—and her hand froze on the mouse. *Why am I doing this? I'm supposed to be letting the police handle it.*

Shannon clicked the browser shut. "I was only curious because Mrs. Reid mentioned that his behavior led her grand-mother to change her will. But it's really none of my business."

"I don't blame her for changing the will if Warren was a thug."

Shannon laid aside Mrs. Reid's partial family tree. If she had time, *maybe* she'd look into it further—purely to satisfy her curiosity. Nothing more. But finishing the restoration on the bag was more urgent, and so was spending time with the twins on their last Saturday evening in Apple Grove.

* * *

Shannon, Alec, and Lara drove together to church on Sunday, but Deborah stayed home, pleading a headache.

"I hope all of the stress from the break-in isn't getting to her," Shannon said as Alec put Old Blue in gear.

"She went to bed early last night," Lara said. "She's been doing a lot for us, helping us get ready for tomorrow."

The reminder that her children would leave home the next day put a slight damper on Shannon's outlook. "We'll have to make sure she takes it easy today. I told her before we left that we'd fix our own lunch, even if it means peanut butter sandwiches."

After Sunday school, Shannon caught herself scanning the pews for Michael's tall, handsome form, but he was nowhere to be seen. *Likely out of town again.* His security business kept him on the road a lot, and he'd told her earlier that late summer and fall were his busiest seasons.

She found a seat with Joyce and Bill Buchanan, while Lara and Alec hurried off to sit with their friends. Near the end of the sermon, Shannon felt her cellphone vibrate in her pocket. She eased it out to glance at the screen and recognized the name at once.

The security company.

Her heart jumped, and she hurried down the aisle and out the door to answer the call before it went to voicemail. "Hello?"

"Mrs. McClain?"

"Yes."

The caller identified himself.

"Is it the store alarm?" she asked.

"No, ma'am. It's your house, I'm afraid."

Shannon's throat tightened. *In broad daylight?*

He continued, "I called the house, and Miss Waters told me to notify the police, so I did that first."

Shannon's mind raced. "Thank you! I'm at church, but I can be home in ten minutes or less."

The church bell rang, and she turned as the double doors opened and people began to stream out. For a moment, she feared it would take her ten minutes just to find the kids, but soon Alec appeared. He stood several inches taller than his companions, his wavy red hair a beacon for Shannon. She waved and caught his attention, beckoning him while summoning up an expression so somber he would have to know it was urgent.

Alec's eyebrows shot up. He turned back for an instant, then emerged from the throng, dragging Lara behind him by the hand. Sidestepping those who'd stopped to speak to the pastor, they scurried down the steps.

"What is it?" Lara asked, out of breath.

"The alarm again, at home."

"Oh, no. Not *again!*"

"Is Deborah OK?" Alec asked.

"I think so." Shannon tossed him the keys. "You drive. I'll call her."

"Right." Alec set his jaw and hustled her and Lara to the truck.

Alec had the truck in motion even before Shannon finished dialing the landline at the Paisley mansion.

On the fifth ring, someone finally answered—a man. "Hello?"

Shannon's pulse tripped. "Who is this?"

"It's Chief Grayson. That you, Shannon?"

She sighed with relief. "Yes. Is Deborah all right?"

"I think so, but I just got here."

"We're on our way home now."

"Good. I'll talk to you then." Grayson hung up, and Shannon clicked her phone off.

"The police are already there," she told the twins.

"Mum, *why* are all these things happening?" Lara asked, using the dash as a brace as Alec sped around the corner into the driveway.

"I don't know, sweetie. And I'm sorry to be putting you through another bad time." Shannon slipped an arm around her shoulder. "I'm sure Grayson will catch whoever's doing it." *And he'd better hurry up about it.*

Lara scoffed. "Scotland is starting to look pretty safe compared to this crazy town."

Alec raced up the driveway and drove right to the front steps. Old Blue lurched to a stop. Lara opened her door, and she and Shannon hopped out. Shannon left her belongings in the truck and sprinted for the front door. "It's locked, Alec—bring my keys!"

Before he could get them to her, Officer Doan opened the door. "Sorry, Mrs. McClain. We entered through the back door."

"Thanks." Shannon pushed in, and he took a step back. She stood in the foyer, looking around. "Where's Deborah?"

"In her room, I think, ma'am."

Shannon strode to the kitchen. Chief Grayson stood beyond the refrigerator, at the closed door to Deborah's quarters, with Officer Brownley standing right behind him.

"Yes, ma'am," Grayson said loudly, beckoning Shannon. "She's here now."

"What happened?" Shannon hurried to his side. "Is she in there?"

Grayson sighed. "Yes. Would you speak to her, please?"

Shannon turned to the door. "Deborah? It's me. Open the door."

There was a moment's silence, and then the lock clicked. The door creaked open a few inches.

Deborah's chalky face appeared in the crack. Her eyes lit up when she saw Shannon. "Thank God!" She flung the door open and wrapped her in a big hug. "I was so frightened."

Shannon put her arms around Deborah. "It's all right now."

The twins hovered in the doorway. The kitchen seemed small with so many people bunched in it.

Grayson gave them a moment and then cleared his throat. "Brownley, go help Doan make a thorough sweep of the house."

Officer Brownley nodded and edged past Alec into the next room.

"Miss Waters, the security company said the back door alarm went off," Grayson said. "Can you tell us what happened?"

Shannon glanced over Deborah's shoulder toward the back entrance and shivered. The door stood open, but from ten feet away, she couldn't see any obvious damage.

Deborah released Shannon, the pallor of shock still evident on her face. She turned to Grayson. "I was starting to get lunch ready." She glanced sharply at Shannon, as though daring her to say she shouldn't have done that. "I heard someone moving around out back, and then the doorknob rattled, like someone tried to open the door. I jumped back, and then I heard something crunch against the door, and the alarm starting ringing. I ran into my bedroom and locked the door, then I got in the bathroom and locked that door too."

Grayson took a few notes as she spoke. "Do you think the perp knew you were in here?"

"I don't know. I just knew I wanted as many doors as I could get between me and whoever it was. After I got in my room, I thought maybe I should have gone out the front door instead, but I was afraid there might be someone out there too. When the phone rang, I crept out of my bathroom and answered the one in my bedroom. The alarm company said they'd call you and Shannon."

"And they did, as you can see." Grayson spoke slowly and kept his voice calm. "What did you do after that?"

"I heard someone walking around out here, so I scooted back into the bathroom and locked the door again. I figured if he got into my bedroom, I'd go out the bathroom window, but I was hoping you'd get here first."

Grayson looked up from his notes. "I take it he never made it that far?"

"No," Deborah said. "I don't know where he went, but I didn't hear him in my room."

Shannon stroked her shoulder. "You did fine, Deborah. I'm so glad you're safe."

Officer Doan came into the kitchen. "The house is clear, Chief."

"You went upstairs?"

"All the way to the attic. It's a big house. There's a locked door on the east corner of the top floor, though. We didn't access that."

"That's the turret room," Shannon said. "It used to be my mother's darkroom, and I keep it locked." If she got the chance to talk to Grayson alone, she would tell him she'd hidden the Art Deco bag there.

"I did notice there's a bit of a mess in the study," Officer Doan said.

As he spoke, Officer Brownley came in. "One of the bedrooms looks disturbed too, Chief."

"That's probably mine. I'm not the neatest person." Lara flashed her signature smile.

Officer Brownley seemed momentarily dazed by it. Clearing his throat, he said, "I thought it was the master bedroom. The dresser drawers are on the floor, their contents scattered all over the place. It looks like it's been ransacked. Not vandalized though."

Lara bristled. "*What?* You mean somebody pawed through Mum's or my clothes?"

"Everybody stay calm," Grayson said. He looked at Lara. "Why don't you fix Miss Waters a cup of tea, please? Shannon, I'd like you to come around with me now and see if anything's missing."

"Sure." She patted Lara's shoulder as she passed and gave Alec a resigned smile.

When they reached the foyer, Grayson said, "Do you have the key to the locked room?"

"It's in my desk upstairs."

He nodded. "It won't hurt to make sure our intruder isn't in there, but I suspect he ran out the way he came in when he saw us pull up."

All of the artworks seemed to be in place in the downstairs rooms. Shannon poked her head in the study, and she gasped.

Her crafting supplies and numerous books lay scattered across the floor. The cheerful yellow walls and bright sunlight streaming through the windows belied the chaos before her.

"Do you still have that purse you showed me at the store the other day?" Grayson asked.

She nodded. "I work on it in this room, but it should be upstairs in the locked turret room. I gave the jeweled pin back to the owner. I'll show you where I keep the bag when we go upstairs."

"OK. Do you think anything's been taken from this

room? I know it's hard to tell when things are in disarray, but since he left the paintings and statuary alone, I suspect he was after your client's antique purse."

Shannon took a quick look at the worktable where the drawers had been opened and rifled. "As far as I can tell, everything is here, just jumbled."

They went upstairs and took a quick look in Alec's room. As usual, it was neat, and his luggage, all packed for his move to the campus, sat untouched, next to the closet door.

They moved on to Lara's doorway.

"This is my daughter's room." The bed wasn't made, and a jacket hung off the side of her purple beanbag chair. A couple of books and a pair of slippers lay haphazardly on the floor, but Shannon didn't think it was overly messy— for Lara. "This looks normal, but Lara can tell you for sure."

"Must have hit the master bedroom, like Brownley said," Grayson muttered.

Shannon led him to her door and gasped. Her beautiful sanctuary had been invaded and turned topsy-turvy. Clothes lay in heaps on the carpet near her dresser. The smaller drawers had been flung aside, and the larger ones hung open. Shannon felt her face flush as she recognized some of her lingerie on top of the pile. The secretary desk near the balcony window had also been rifled, and her pens and stationery were strewn about. The bedclothes hung off the end of the bed, and pillows lay on the floor.

"Is that the bathroom?" Grayson nodded toward it.

"Yes." Shannon stepped to it and looked inside. One of the potted African violets from the windowsill had been knocked over, spilling its potting soil on the tile floor, and the medicine cabinet door hung open. "Other than the mess, everything looks like it should."

Grayson joined her. "Do you keep any prescription medicines in here?"

"No. There was aspirin and motion sickness pills— over-the-counter stuff."

"What's in there?" He walked out of the bathroom toward the door of her walk-in closet.

Shannon followed him and opened it. Her hanging clothes had been pushed aside, and several handbags from a shelf had been thrown down onto the floor.

"There's no doubt about it. He—or she—is looking for something specific," Grayson said.

"Yes." Shannon swallowed hard and glanced around the room again. "I didn't notice those before." She gestured toward a small watercolor painting and sampler lying on the floor in the corner near the bed. Empty picture hooks still protruded from the wall above them. "Do you think he was going to steal those?"

Grayson rubbed his chin. "No. I think he was looking for a wall safe."

"But I don't have one."

"He didn't know that. It's probably a good thing you don't. I have a feeling he came prepared to open one."

Shannon shook her head with dismay. "He knew this was my room. He didn't bother with the kids' things."

Grayson looked around, his face sober. "It's obviously the master bedroom."

"Still …" She frowned up at him. "I think whoever did this

has been watching us and knows we all leave the mansion for two or three hours on Sunday mornings."

"That could be." Grayson took out his notebook and jotted a note in it.

She walked to the secretary and stuck her hand into one of the pigeonholes to release a catch. A panel slid back, revealing a small hiding place where she kept the turret room key.

"Well, well." Grayson eyed her with respect. "That's very clever. He didn't find that either."

"My grandmother had lots of little secrets. Something tells me I haven't discovered them all yet. Follow me."

Shannon led him down the hall and up the winding stairs to the door of the turret room and unlocked it. "I hope to clean this out someday and fix it up. It used to be my mom's darkroom."

Grayson looked around the small space. "Interesting."

"That was years and years ago, when Beth—my mom— lived here. Give me one second." Shannon knelt on the floor and pried up the loose tile. She took out the beaded bag, which she'd wrapped securely in tissue paper and a plastic bag. "Here it is."

Grayson took it and glanced inside the sack. "Seems OK to me."

Shannon nodded. "I'm sure no one's touched it."

"Good. The fact that several valuable items in the house were ignored, added to the obvious search that was made in your room and the study, confirms my theory that the thief was looking for one thing, and he most likely didn't find it. The bag."

Shannon gritted her teeth and let the "my theory" comment slide—certain she'd been the first one to suggest it. "So where should I keep it? It's not convenient to put it in a bank safe. I need access to it so I can finish the job and get it back to the owner as soon as possible."

"Keep it in here when you're not working on it." Grayson pointed to the loose tile. "Put it back under there and lock this door again."

Shannon thought about it and wasn't able to come up with a better alternative. "I'll do that—and I'll be careful not to sit in front of any windows with it. I don't want to advertise that it's still in here." She replaced the package and the loose tile, then stood and brushed off her knees. "After you, Chief."

As they walked back to the staircase, Grayson asked, "What else can you tell me about that bag?"

Shannon gave him a brief rundown of the designer and workmanship, the vintage beads she'd special-ordered for the repair, and the appraised value Mrs. Reid had mentioned. She also told him about returning the jeweled pin to the owner.

"Hmm." Grayson paused on the landing and took out his notebook. "Possibly the thief was after the pin rather than the bag."

Shannon blinked up at him. "But ... that would mean he'd know it was hidden inside."

"Yes. You said yourself that it couldn't have gotten in there by accident."

"True." Shannon thought about it for a moment. "There's Mrs. Reid's cousin too. He has a criminal record."

"Who's that?" Grayson eyed her keenly.

Shannon filled him in on Warren Tuttle.

"You knew all this and didn't think to tell me?" Grayson demanded, his voice taking on the typical gruff tone Shannon was used to hearing—especially in statements aimed at her.

She stepped back and folded her arms across her chest. "I didn't know it the last time I saw you. Mrs. Reid told me the history when she came to get the pin."

"Tuttle." Grayson wrote the name in his notebook. "So he was on the naughty list, and Grandma disinherited him."

"He still got something. 'A small bequest,' is how Mrs. Reid put it. But nothing as valuable as the bag or the pin."

"Can you give me this Mrs. Reid's full name and address?"

Shannon gave him what information she had stored in her cellphone.

"I'll look into it," Grayson said, his demeanor softening again.

"There is one other thing. Right after you left the store the other day, Chloe Kitchener came in. She didn't stop at the counter or anything. In fact, we're not even sure she entered through the front door. She came right to my office, and she saw me holding Mrs. Reid's bag."

Grayson's eyes narrowed. "You don't say. I'll have another chat with Chloe."

"You don't honestly think she could be mixed up in this, do you?"

Grayson took out a handkerchief and dabbed at his sweaty forehead. "This whole mess with the break-ins, Fredo's sketches, and his murder is so bizarre, I think *anything* is possible at this point. I suspect Chloe is simply an opportunist. If you left something lying around where she could pilfer it, she wouldn't hesitate. But to break into someone's house and look for it—I'm not sure. It's certainly worth following up on though. I'll put her on notice that she's on my radar. If she shows up at the store again, let me know right away."

"I will." Shannon clutched the railing and looked down into the foyer. "I'll be worried about Deborah every day now when I go to the store."

"We'll catch this guy."

"Will you?" She looked up into his eyes, her gaze a silent challenge. "I hope you do—before someone else gets hurt."

Grayson narrowed his eyes but said nothing.

"I've got to take the twins to Portland tomorrow. Deborah will be here alone. What if he comes back?"

"Then either Deborah or the alarm company will call us."

"Brilliant," Shannon said flatly.

Grayson sighed. "I'm doing all I can. Look, this Tuttle fellow sounds like a good lead. I'll be looking at him closely, you can be sure."

Below them, Alec and Lara appeared in the foyer.

"Mum, is everything OK up there?" Alec asked.

"Yes, it's fine. My room's a little mussed, but it's nothing serious, and I don't think anything was taken."

"I don't get it." Alec frowned and shook his head. "What did he want?"

Shannon glanced at Grayson, but before she could speak, Lara piped up.

"It's that bag, isn't it? Mrs. Reid said it was valuable."

Shannon walked down the steps, and Grayson followed.

"We don't know." Shannon went to Lara and touched her shoulder. "If it was, then he left here sorely disappointed, because he didn't find it."

"You really think that's what the bloke was after?" Alec asked.

"It very well may be," Grayson said.

"Told you." Lara gave her brother a superior nod.

Alec frowned. "I haven't even gotten to see it."

"Sorry. I didn't suppose you'd be interested." Shannon turned to Grayson. "All right, what now?"

"Let me check with my officers and see if they've found anything outside. We'll take a look at the back entrance to see if it needs repairs too."

"Och, the insurance company is going to love hearing from me again so soon." Shannon ran a hand through her hair.

Deborah poked her head around the corner. "Is anyone hungry? Because lunch is ready."

Shannon and the twins looked at Grayson.

"Go ahead," he said. "I think we're about done here, but I'll let you know if we need anything else. I'll check out the lead you gave me. And I meant what I said, Shannon. We'll catch this guy."

He marched back to the kitchen, and Shannon put one arm around Alec and the other around Lara.

"Come on, let's eat."

"I'm not hungry," Lara said.

"Well, I am." Alec strode into the dining room.

"Come on, sweetie," Shannon said softly to Lara. "After all Deborah's been through, she made us a nice lunch. Let's support her by enjoying it."

Lara sighed. "All right. I'll try."

*   *   *

Later that afternoon, Betty called. "I saw you and the kids leave the church pretty fast, and I wanted to make sure everything's all right."

"Yes, thank you," Shannon said. "The house alarm went off—but everything is OK now. Grayson and his men came." She wondered how much she ought to tell Betty over the phone. Betty was a good friend, and Shannon longed to pour out the entire story to her, but not when one of the children might overhear how truly worried she was.

"Tomorrow's the day the kids leave, isn't it?" Betty asked.

"Yes. I'm taking them to Portland in the morning." Shannon's spirits drooped just thinking about it—but the way things were going in Apple Grove, the twins might actually be safer at school.

"I could take them," Betty offered. "So you wouldn't have to be away from the store."

"Aw, thanks. That's sweet of you, but ..." Shannon looked over her shoulder to make sure she was alone in the drawing room at that moment. "I don't want to give up my last hour of 'Mum time' with them."

Betty chuckled. "I understand. But it's going to be a lonesome drive home afterward, you know. Would you like for me to come along?"

"I'd love that. You could keep me company and stop me from crying on the way back."

"You got it."

Shannon spent much of the afternoon putting her bedroom, bath, and closet back in order. After supper, she retrieved the Art Deco bag and took it to the study. She closed the drapes before she set out the containers of special beads. She laid her scissors, needle case, and the small skein of silk thread on the table and then turned on the lamp and took out her reading glasses for the close work.

Handling the beads was a joy, and she began to hum softly as she worked, painstakingly choosing the exact one for each spot. The restoration was more than half done, and soon she would be able to return the bag to its owner. But the more she thought about it, the more she began to worry about Mrs. Reid. *After I return the bag, will the thief target her next?*

As she thought about the bag's long history, she pictured the scene Mrs. Reid had described—with her cousin Warren demanding the bag and trying to take it from her. The woman had done well to hang on to it and gather up most of the tiny beads after he had gone. As she slid the point of her needle through two gray-green beads and a mottled green-and-black one, Shannon hoped her labor would bring it back to the beautiful object in the painting from 1935.

"Is that what the burglar wanted?"

"Och!" Shannon jumped and looked up to find Alec standing next to her chair. "I didn't hear you come in."

"Sorry. I didn't mean to startle you. I was just curious. That little thing is worth a fortune?"

Shannon smiled. "A small fortune, perhaps."

"It seems like a weird thing to make such a fuss over." Alec sighed. "Some people will do anything for money."

Shannon thought about her thief. *Would he do anything— including murder?*

— 16 —

On Monday morning, Shannon rose early, but Deborah was already up preparing a huge breakfast and loading "care packages" of cookies for the twins to take with them.

"How's the headache?" Shannon asked.

Deborah snorted. "It's gone—the burglar scared it right out of me, I think."

"I'm glad." Shannon set the breakfast table. To her surprise, the twins needed no prodding and carried their luggage downstairs in plenty of time for the meal.

Shannon was too nervous to eat much, but Alec seemed to have no problem putting away two plates full of waffles, bacon, and applesauce.

Lara flitted about, full of energy. She sat down to eat twice, but each time remembered something she wanted to fetch from another part of the house, and dashed away. Finally, she downed one waffle and a cup of tea and insisted that was all she wanted. "I'll help you load the dishwasher, Deborah," she said with a grin at the housekeeper.

Deborah waved her offer away. "I don't need any help."

"I want to." Lara pouted. "I won't get another chance for a while, and I wanted to say thank you for making us such a super breakfast."

"It *is* extra good," Alec agreed, reaching for the syrup pitcher.

Deborah gave in, and she and Lara began clearing dirty dishes. Shannon lingered over her tea, trying not to dwell on the fact that it was the twins' last meal at home for a while. Despite her stalling, the time came when they needed to leave. They planned to take Deborah's car and pick up Betty at the inn.

It took three trips to the garage to load all of the twins' luggage and boxes. Once they squeezed everything into the trunk, Shannon got behind the wheel.

Alec and Lara hugged Deborah and promised they'd see her soon.

As they rode down the long driveway, Lara let out a big sigh. "I'll really miss this place."

"Good. I want you to visit often," Shannon teased.

At The Apple Grove Inn, Shannon pulled up near the front entrance of the rambling yellow Queen Anne house. Before she could put the car in park, Betty stepped out the door.

"Good morning," Betty sang out as she slid into the front passenger seat.

"Hi," Shannon said, already thankful to have her cheerful friend along. She set out down Meadowlark Street, toward the highway.

"Boy, have we got a lot of guests right now," Betty said. "We were full up over the weekend, but some of them are leaving today."

"Will Tom be all right without you there to help?" Shannon asked.

"Oh, sure. Most folks have eaten already, but he'll keep the kitchen open until ten."

Betty's chatter, coupled with the kids' excitement, kept the mood in the car light, and Shannon was surprised at how fast the drive flew by. They arrived on campus shortly after nine o'clock and located Lara's dormitory. Her eyes sparkled as she towed her suitcases up the walkway. Alec followed close behind, carrying her box of textbooks, Betty wheeled a smaller suitcase, and Shannon carried Lara's pillow and extra blanket.

As they reached the lobby of the dorm, Shannon's cellphone rang. She handed off the blanket to Betty and balanced the pillow on top of the box Alec carried so she could get to her phone. The display told her it was Essie, whom she'd left with Melanie in the store for the morning.

"Is anything wrong?" Shannon asked after greeting her.

"No. I just wanted to check with you—a Mr. Lee called. He said he spoke to you last week about renting a loft."

"I did get a call from a gentleman who was interested, and I told him to call back later. I'm not sure of his name, though. That could be the same man."

"He saw the ad in the paper too, and he wants to come see the loft today," Essie said. "Is that all right? I told him I'd call him right back."

Shannon hesitated. "Yes, I suppose it's fine. The police have finished what they needed to do in the studio."

"Then I'll tell him to come when it's convenient."

Shannon ended the call and hurried to catch up with the others.

Lara's roommate had already arrived and was putting away her clothes. Her face lit up when she saw Lara. "Well, hi! I'm Patsy Barlow."

A few inches shorter than Lara, Patsy had light brown

hair and hazel eyes, and her sunny smile never seemed to quit. Within seconds of meeting each other, the girls began discussing their majors, the furniture, their decorations, and plans to go shopping for matching bedspreads and curtains.

Shannon and Betty watched them with amusement. Alec stood by with his hands shoved into his pockets.

Finally, Lara seemed to remember their presence. "I guess you all want to go, huh?"

"Not really," Shannon said, "but we do need to get Alec to his dorm, and it sounds like you and Patsy have lots to talk about."

Patsy grinned. "We're going to get along great!"

"Call me later if you need anything," Alec told his sister.

Lara gave Shannon a final hug. "Mum, we're going to be fine. I know I'm going to like it here." She paused and her expression clouded over. "It's you and Deborah that I'm worried about."

"There is no need to worry about us. We'll be just fine." Shannon squeezed her close for a moment and then let go. "I'm glad you like it here. Call me anytime. I mean it."

"You know I will," Lara said.

Shannon nodded and smiled at Patsy. "Nice to meet you."

A minute later, she was back in the car with Betty and Alec, crawling down a street crowded with students and their parents unloading luggage, bicyclists, an occasional skateboarder, and dozens of other slow-moving vehicles.

Alec's choice of accommodations was a dorm for science, engineering, math, and technology students, where Shannon was sure he would fit right in. He'd also requested a "quiet floor," and she thought that was a wise choice. He'd had one year at St. Andrews and knew how distracting other students could be. On the quiet floor, he would be assured of peace when he needed to study. When he saw his small but well-appointed room, he nodded in satisfaction.

"You didn't want a roommate?" Betty asked.

"I thought I'd try this," Alec said. "If it's too quiet, I'll get one next year."

Moving him in took far less time than it had to get Lara settled. Shannon lingered and offered to help him make up his bed.

"Sure, Mum."

Alec pitched in with quick efficiency. The tasks Shannon could help with were soon complete, and she knew it was time to leave. Several things popped into her mind, including reminders she could give him—"keep your phone charged, check your online banking site often, call me"—but she held them back. *He'll be fine.*

He smiled at her and held out his arms. Shannon hugged him around the waist, trying to hold back her tears.

"Love you," she said.

"I love you too, Mum." Alec released her and looked over at Betty. "Thanks for coming, Mrs. Russo."

Betty smiled. "I'm glad I could. You have a wonderful semester, Alec. I expect I'll see you again soon."

Shannon made it all the way to the stairs before her vision clouded with tears, and she had to wipe her eyes with her sleeve.

Her friend slipped an arm around her shoulders and gave her a squeeze. "I'm proud of you. I know that was hard."

Shannon took a deep breath and pulled herself together. "Thanks, Betty."

They stepped out into sunshine, and a bright blue bird with a black head zipped past Shannon to land on a nearby rhododendron bush.

"What is that bird? They're beautiful!"

"That's called a Steller's jay," Betty said. "It's a kind of blue jay. Haven't you ever seen one before?"

"Yes, in the garden at the mansion, but I never remember to ask Deborah what it is."

"They can be pests." Betty scowled at it. "They drive other birds away from my bird feeder in winter. But you're right, they are pretty."

Sort of like Fredo Benson, Shannon reflected. Bold and different, Fredo had demanded attention. He'd been a pain in some ways—but he'd also had a fine-tuned artistic side.

As they settled in for the drive home, Betty said, "I could see that Alec is a little concerned about you."

"I'm afraid so." Shannon smiled ruefully. "He hates to leave me and Deborah 'unprotected' in the house."

"Chief Grayson *must* have some solid leads by now." Betty pursed her lips. "They need to catch that guy soon. I was shocked when you told me he was bold enough to break into your house in broad daylight—and with your alarm set too."

"It's a little scary," Shannon admitted. "But we think we know what he wanted now, and he'd probably planned on another quick foray into the mansion to snatch it. However, I had it hidden away in a place he couldn't find. The good news—for me—is I won't have it much longer."

"What do you mean?"

"It's the beaded bag I brought to the last Purls meeting. I'm restoring it for a customer. Chief Grayson and I both think that's what the thief is trying to steal. As soon as I finish the beading job, it goes straight back to the owner. I do hope the chief catches the thief first. I'd hate to hear later that the lady who owns it was attacked, or that the bag was stolen from her. I will warn her to be on alert."

Betty eyed her with concern. "*You* need to be careful."

Shannon smiled. "Thanks. Everybody's telling me that. Now you see what Alec is worried about."

The drive went quickly, and Shannon dropped off Betty at the inn before going home for lunch. Deborah had sandwiches ready, and after they ate together, Shannon drove Old Blue to the store. Throwing herself into a busy afternoon's work was a relief. It kept her from thinking how quiet the house would be that evening.

Mr. Lee had come during Shannon's absence and had rented the loft on the spot, Essie reported. "Isn't that great?" she asked.

Shannon agreed, but she couldn't help recalling how Mr. Lee had phoned right after Fredo's death. *Had he known a space would be available soon? What if the person who broke into the store and my house has decided to rent space from me to simplify his mission?*

She shook off the thought when Essie put Mr. Lee's card in her hand. It looked expensive, with raised lettering and a copper-toned spray of wheat near one edge.

"Did he give references?"

"Yes," Essie said. "I called the first one—it's a gallery in Forest Grove. They spoke very highly of him. But then it got busy, and I didn't have time to check the other one."

"Thanks. I'll take care of it."

Essie held out Mr. Lee's application. "I told him he could move in tomorrow. Should I have asked him to wait?"

Shannon blew out a breath. *I have to stop being so suspicious.* "No, that's fine. I'll try to speak with his other reference now."

The second reference was Mr. Lee's employer at a local hospital. He also gave Mr. Lee a glowing recommendation. "I'm afraid we'll lose him if his art catches on," he told Shannon. "He hasn't given up his day job yet, and I'm thankful."

Satisfied, Shannon looked forward to meeting her newest tenant.

*　*　*

Beating the blues was Shannon's main goal on Tuesday. She was determined to keep so busy that she wouldn't think about the children's absence. That resolution prompted her to work on her silver jewelry while she was at the store.

She loved the silversmithing craft she'd learned since coming to Oregon, and her jewelry sold fairly well in the store. Essie claimed they could sell as much as she could make, but Shannon refused to let it take over all her free time. She wanted it to stay an enjoyable hobby.

She finished two pendants and was about to take a break when her cellphone rang. When she saw the name on the caller ID her spirits soared, and she couldn't answer it fast enough.

"Coleen! I'm so glad you called."

"Och, why's that? You've got something juicy to tell me? Something about that handsome Michael Stone?"

Shannon laughed. "Not hardly. Where do you come up with your ridiculous notions?"

"They're not ridiculous," Coleen said. "You know how much I like him. I think he'd be a brilliant match for you."

Shannon felt her cheeks flush, and she glanced nervously over her shoulder—as if anyone else could possibly hear Coleen's side of the conversation. "I'm sorry to disappoint you, but he is *not* the reason I'm so happy to hear from you. I took the twins to Portland yesterday to start the new semester." She paused, fighting the lump that threatened to form in her throat. "I miss them something fierce—and it's only been a day."

"Ah, I'm so sorry to hear that, love. I know how empty the house can feel when they leave. I wish I was there to cheer you up—I'd find us some kind of trouble to mix ourselves up in, you know, take your mind off things," Coleen teased.

Shannon scoffed. "As luck would have it, I'm already mixed up in a troublesome situation without your help."

"For goodness' sake, don't leave me in the dark. Do tell."

Shannon filled her in on Fredo's sketches, his murder, and the break-ins. "I'm afraid Chief Grayson is still no closer to solving any of it than he was two weeks ago."

"Grayson?" Coleen blurted out his name with irritation. "You mean *the* Chief Grayson who was of absolutely no help to you when you first arrived in Oregon? The same Grayson who stood by and did nothing while you were being threatened by a lunatic who would've rather seen you dead than let you claim your inheritance?"

Shannon hesitated. "I'm not sure that's exactly how it happened, but yes, that Grayson."

"You're leaving it up to *him* to get to the bottom of all of this?"

"I am."

Coleen huffed out a breath. "Who is this? What impostor redhead answered my dear friend Shannon McClain's phone?"

"C'mon Coleen, you know it's me. And your description of our police chief isn't quite accurate. He works hard to keep the residents of this town safe."

"But I can't understand why you aren't looking into matters yourself. They involve you, your home, and your business, after all."

"You weren't here to see how horribly the recent murder of Alton Percy affected Lara," Shannon said, feeling defensive. "The investigation nearly got Lara and Alec killed! As long as the kids are living under my roof, I'm not getting any more involved than absolutely necessary in matters best left to the police. Period."

Coleen remained silent for a few moments. "I understand what you're saying. But I do have one teensy question for you."

"What?" Shannon snapped.

"Where are the kids now?"

"Coleen! You're not listening to me. I just told you I took them to Portland yesterday to ..." Shannon's voice trailed off as she caught Coleen's drift.

"Exactly," Coleen said. "They're safe and sound in Portland. No more feeling guilty about putting them in harm's way *should* you decide to do a little investigating on your own."

Shannon blinked. "My goodness, you're right! I don't have to sit around with my stomach in a knot, waiting for the next bad thing to happen anymore—praying that it doesn't." She felt as if a huge weight had been lifted off her shoulders. "I am *not* a victim. And I *don't* want to give the bag back to Mrs. Reid knowing it will make her the new target."

Coleen chuckled. "That's my girl. What are you waiting for?"

"Oh, Coleen, thank you. This was just the pep talk I needed today."

"On that note, I'll let you go. It sounds like you have a lot to do. Give that delicious Michael Stone a big hug and a peck on the cheek for me, will you?"

Shannon smiled. "No. But I'll tell him you said hi."

"Spoilsport."

As soon as they ended their call, Shannon dialed Betty, Joyce, Melanie, and Kate and called an emergency lunch meeting of the Purls. An idea had begun to form in Shannon's mind, a way to catch the thief red-handed—but she'd need her friends help.

The thief is not going to terrorize me anymore.

— 17 —

By closing time, Shannon was nearly bursting with anticipation. She could hardly wait until she and the Purls could put their plan in motion.

She and Essie quickly made the last rounds of the store, straightening displays and returning misplaced items to their proper locations. Artists who'd been working in their lofts drifted downstairs and left for the night. Carrie finished cleaning up in the coffee shop and headed out, while Shannon balanced the day's receipts and put the cash in the safe. The take was so large she wished she'd made an extra run to the bank before it closed.

Once everything was shut down and put away for the night, she and Essie went out the back door.

"Good night," Essie called as she got into her car.

"See you tomorrow." Shannon had one foot inside Old Blue when Michael's black Lexus pulled up next to her.

He got out and flashed a crooked smile across the top of his car. "I guess you're heading home."

"Yes. Good work, detective," she teased, but she removed her foot and walked toward the back of the truck.

He joined her near the bumper. "I just got back in town. Thought I'd swing by here on my way home and see how you're doing."

"I'm hanging in there." Shannon glanced over her

shoulder. Essie shot her a sly smile through her car window as she pulled away.

"Did you get Alec and Lara off to school all right?"

Shannon nodded with a little grimace. "Betty and I took them yesterday."

"How's Alec doing?"

"He's fine, as far as I can tell. You know, Lara shows every emotion she feels clear as day for the world to see, and she was bubbling over all day yesterday. But Alec tends to hold in his feelings more. I think he was just as excited as Lara though." She pushed a lock of hair back from her face. "I know he's eager to start his science classes. He says the university's laboratories are awesome."

Michael rested one foot on the bumper. "That's right, he's a biology major, isn't he?"

"Yes. He's always had a scientific bent. When he was little, he liked to dig up my garden to see if the seeds had sprouted. It made growing anything next to impossible."

Michael laughed. "I'm not sure if I should tell you this or not, but he called me yesterday."

"In Timbuktu?"

"Tokyo. When I talked to him before, about the murder, I gave him my cellphone number, told him to use it any-time."

"That was nice of you." Shannon hesitated. "Do I dare ask what time it was when he called—or why, for that matter?"

Michael studied her with serious blue eyes. "He called to talk about you."

"Me?"

"He asked me if I'd check in on you now and then, since

he's not living in Apple Grove anymore. I assured him I was already planning on it."

Shannon felt her face flush. "He's a sweet kid—well on his way to becoming a tender, thoughtful man."

Michael nodded. "So, how *are* you? Have things settled down at all?"

"Yes and no. We had an incident at the house Sunday. I don't know if you heard about it."

He rubbed the back of his neck. "I just touched down in Portland this afternoon, and all I know is the bit that Alec shared with me." Michael's company, Stone & McCrary Security Consultants, had corporate clients all over the world, and Shannon knew he spent a lot of time traveling.

"Someone broke into the house while the kids and I were at church," she said. "Deborah was at home. The alarm system worked, but the burglar still went in through the back door."

Michael's eyebrows shot up. "While the alarm was sounding?"

"That's right. We don't think he realized Deborah was home. She locked herself in her bedroom and answered the phone when the security people called. They alerted the police and then me."

"Did they catch him?"

"No. The police got there before I did, but the burglar was gone. Grayson thinks the intruder counted on having several minutes to ransack the place before they arrived."

"How bad was it?"

"The study and my bedroom were targeted and torn apart."

Michael's eyes narrowed. "Sounds like your burglar knew exactly what he was after."

"That's our conclusion. And now we think we know what it is he wants."

"Care to tell me?"

Shannon gazed up into his vivid blue eyes and her breath caught. Coleen's word, *delicious*, floated stubbornly through her mind. Michael's presence seemed to be working its magic on her. *Should I tell him about my plan to catch the thief?*

She gave herself a mental shake and looked away briefly to break the connection. "We think the thief is after an old, museum-quality beaded bag that I'm restoring for a client."

Michael gave a low whistle. "Do you know if Grayson has any suspects?"

"He doesn't have a clue." Her statement came out harsher than she'd intended, and she softened her tone. "He's trying; I know he is. Currently, he's focusing on the bag owner's family, particularly a cousin. And he located a couple of men who were in prison with Fredo Benson. He emailed me their mug shots so I'd recognize them if they showed up in the store or at my house. But his efforts have not deterred the thief in the slightest."

Michael thought for a moment. "So Grayson thinks Fredo's jail mates may have been in on a deal with him, then turned on him and killed him?"

"I'm not sure if that's what he thinks exactly," Shannon said, "but he did tell me Fredo was dead before the store was broken into."

Michael nodded. "And now someone's broken into your house twice, if I'm counting right."

"Twice that we know about. Fredo broke into my house multiple times before he died to take pictures." Shannon shuddered as she recalled the disturbing sketches and photos of her private residence.

"If Fredo knew how to bypass your home alarm, you'd think his buddies would too, and they wouldn't set it off or ignore it while they searched your house."

Shannon leaned against the tailgate. "I've thought about that, and I don't have an explanation, unless Fredo got in before we were as diligent about using the alarm as we should've been. It does make my client's cousin seem like a more likely suspect in comparison. Chief Grayson said he'd look into that angle, but I haven't heard back from him."

"I'll talk to Grayson about it and see what I can find out."

Shannon smiled. "Thanks." She jangled her keys nervously at her side, struggling to decide whether or not to let him in on her plan. *He might tell Grayson.*

Michael glanced at her jingling keys. "I should let you get going." But instead of moving away, he leaned in toward her. Her hand froze. "For the record, I really *would* have stopped by, even if Alec hadn't asked me to." He casually removed his foot from the bumper.

"That's good to know," she managed to squeak out, her voice barely above a whisper.

He stepped aside and she darted to Old Blue's door without so much as a backward glance. Once on the highway and out of his sight, she felt a smile creep across her face.

It stayed there all the way home.

— 18 —

Shannon didn't see Michael again for two days. Although plotting with the Purls to catch the thief and work had kept her busy, she thought of him often and wondered if he'd spoken to Grayson about the case. By Thursday morning, she speculated that he'd been called out of town again, and she felt more than a little dismayed by the thought.

But shortly after lunch, he sauntered into the store. "Busy place." He flashed the grin that always made her heart flutter.

"It is." She finished merchandising the last skein of angora in the yarn section and stood. "I'm ready for a coffee break. How about you?"

"Sounds good."

He followed her into the coffee shop, where a half dozen people sat enjoying their beverages.

Melanie smiled at them from behind the counter. "Hey, Michael. I haven't seen you for a while."

"I've been on the road more than I'd like. How are you doing?"

"Very well, thanks to my friends." Melanie cast a fond glance at Shannon.

"I'm glad to hear that," Michael said. "I'll take a small black coffee, please. Shannon, what'll you have?"

"*Plain* black coffee?" Melanie frowned at him in mock dismay. "Be a little adventurous. How about a caramel latté?"

Shannon chuckled and said, "I'd like a large vanilla cappuccino."

"OK, give me one of those too." Michael cocked an eyebrow at Melanie. "Or isn't that adventurous enough?"

Melanie pursed her lips. "It's a step in the right direction. Two vanilla cappuccinos coming up."

Melanie fixed their drinks, and Shannon and Michael carried them to a small table in the corner.

"I'm beginning to think I might like coffee better than tea," she told him in a conspiratorial tone. "I can't believe I just said that out loud."

"Your secret is safe with me." He winked and took an experimental sip. "This isn't bad, although I'm still not sure it qualifies as coffee."

"So what have you been up to?" Shannon asked.

"Other than business as usual, I did a little digging on those two ex-cons you mentioned—Fredo Benson's former jail mates."

"Find anything interesting?"

He shrugged. "Maybe. One of them left the area as soon as he was sprung. He's been living near Chicago, and Grayson is pretty sure he hasn't been back to Oregon in the last month."

Disappointed, Shannon set down her drink. "That rules him out for Fredo's murder and the break-ins then."

"The other guy's staying in the Portland area. He seems to have gone back to his pre-jail girlfriend."

"Hmm. Any chance he was in Apple Grove around the first of the month?"

"He says not, but he can't prove it," Michael said.

"You actually talked to him?"

"I did. This morning."

Shannon felt as if the breath had been squeezed from her lungs. "Just like that? You went to Portland and confronted him?"

"With Grayson's approval. His name's Hank Goodson."

"He's the surly-looking one." Shannon recalled the mug shot. Her mental image was of a dark-haired man of about thirty with close-set eyes, a scraggly beard, and a contemptuous expression for the camera.

"No one takes a good mug shot."

"Sort of like driver's license photos?"

Michael laughed. "Guess so. Anyway, Goodson says he's never been to Apple Grove, but I don't know. He's got a rap sheet a mile long, and his offenses include breaking and entering."

Shannon raised her eyebrows. "Does he steal safes?"

"Not that I know of."

"It sounds to me like Hank would have grabbed anything valuable if he'd gotten into my house, and not concentrated on searching for just one thing."

Michael sat back with a slight smile twisting his lips. "He did tell me an interesting story about Fredo Benson. Your Van Gogh wannabe—seems he didn't mutilate his ear for art after all."

"Oh?" Shannon took a sip. "That's almost comforting. What did Hank say about it?"

"There was a fight in the exercise yard. Someone had it in for Benson and jumped him. They scuffled, and before the guards could stop it, Benson lost a chunk of his ear. They say the other guy bit it off."

Shannon gasped. "How bizarre! Why would Fredo say he did it himself?"

"Maybe he thought it sounded more romantic than getting bested in a jailhouse brawl."

She wrinkled her face. "I almost wish you hadn't told me. I wonder if Grayson's followed up on Lois Reid's cousin, Warren Tuttle."

"He's the man who was supposed to inherit the valuable heirloom that happens to be in your possession, right?"

Shannon nodded. "That's right. He has a criminal record too."

"According to Grayson, he was never in the same facility as Fredo Benson. No connection has been found between them yet. But Grayson's looking at him for the break-ins."

"Maybe Fredo's murder has nothing to do with those." Shannon glanced around the coffee shop. Most of the customers were gone, and the only couple remaining was deep in conversation.

"There's got to be a connection," Michael said. "You don't get coincidences like that."

"Don't you? What if Fredo had an argument with a girlfriend—or some girlfriend's former boyfriend? People kill for many reasons besides money."

Michael fell silent for a moment, gazing down into his mug. When he looked up, he smiled. "The police are looking into it. That's all I can say. You know Grayson's a thorough investigator."

Shannon looked away, avoiding his gaze. "I know he's doing his best. But the sooner the burglar is caught, the better."

*   *   *

That evening, Lara called, very excited. "Would you mind terribly if Alec and I didn't come home this weekend? A group of students is going to drive up the Columbia Gorge. They say there are awesome things to see—waterfalls and dams and old steamboats."

Shannon had to smile, despite her disappointment. "That sounds like a wonderful opportunity for you."

"Are you sure it's all right, Mum?"

"Yes, you go ahead. But I hope I'll get to see you both Labor Day weekend."

"Of course you will. We were all set to come tomorrow night, but then this came up. We'll be taking a school van and making a day of it on Saturday."

"Call me when you get back to your dorm?" Shannon asked.

"I'll do that. Thanks, Mum. You're the best."

Shannon fought off the loneliness that hit when they hung up. *It's best they don't come home this weekend,* she thought, reflecting on her plans. *Who knows what the next few days may bring?*

Returning her attention to the task at hand, she retrieved Mrs. Reid's bag from its hiding place in the turret and took it to the study. She flipped on every light in the room—and left the shades wide open.

As she arranged her tools on the worktable in front of the window, Deborah poked her head in the door.

"Everyone is in position and ready," she said, her expression tense with anticipation. "Are you doing OK?"

Shannon nodded. "I just hope our persistent burglar is watching and we catch him on the first try. I'd hate to have to go through this every night for a week or more."

"You know the Purls and I wouldn't mind one bit if that's what it takes to put a stop to all of this nonsense. It's high time someone catches the troublemaker. I'm tired of living in fear, wondering when he might strike again and knowing he probably will as long as that bag is in the house."

"I agree." Shannon's gaze dropped to the antique beaded bag on the table. "And I wouldn't feel right about simply hurrying to finish my repairs so I could get the bag out of my house. All I'd be doing is passing the problem on to Mrs. Reid, likely putting her in danger."

Deborah smiled. "You're a good woman, Shannon." She ducked out of the room, and Shannon got to work on repairing the bag.

For the next two hours, she worked with trembling fingers, wondering if her burglar watched from the darkness beyond her window. When her cellphone buzzed to alert her of a text message, it startled her so much she nearly poked herself with the needle.

With her heart still racing, she read Betty's group text message: "Intruder spotted in back garden. Dressed in black with ski mask. Can't see face. Heading toward side of mansion."

Shannon's breath caught. *This is it. This is actually happening.* She sent up a silent prayer that Betty would remain safely hidden at her post behind the summer house.

Willing her pulse to slow, she continued her work, miraculously managing to thread a bead over her needle with quivering hands. Was she foolish to have acted on this plan with her friends? *What if he has a gun and all we have are cans of mace?*

Her phone buzzed again; this time it was a message from Joyce. "Target hiding in trees near study window."

It was too late to scuttle the plan now. Shannon fought the urge to turn her head toward the window. *Not that I could see much in the dark.* With great fanfare, she yawned and stretched, then laid the bag on the table in front of the window. She turned off the lights and walked out of the room, leaving the shades wide open, as she and the others had agreed.

As she approached the foyer, Deborah's head peeked out from around a corner in the kitchen hall. "The alarm is off and all doors are unlocked," she whispered.

Shannon took a deep breath. "Good. I'll be back down shortly." She went upstairs and turned on her bedroom light. She waited a few minutes before turning it off again so the burglar would think she'd gone to bed. Then she grabbed her small can of mace, crept back downstairs in the dark, and hid in the drawing room.

Her phone buzzed in her pocket as another text came through, and she quickly turned the ringer from vibrate to silent.

She read Kate's message: "Company's coming. Melanie, call police now."

Had they waited too long to make the call? Shannon wished she had the assurance that Grayson was already on his way.

To Shannon's hyper-alert ears, the barely audible click

of the front doorknob being turned sounded like a gunshot. *Stay calm. You can't fall apart now.*

Soft footsteps sounded in the foyer, advancing slowly toward her. They paused briefly outside the entrance to the drawing room, where Shannon hid just inside the open door, before moving on.

Shannon swallowed hard and tiptoed from her hiding place to follow the dark form down the shadowy hall leading to the study. She gripped her can of mace tightly, praying no harm would come to any of her friends as they carried out the rest of their plan.

When the intruder slipped into the study, Shannon quickened her pace to catch up, stopping just outside the door to gather her nerve.

Out of the corner of her eye, she saw Deborah creeping down the hall toward her. *It's now or never.* She raised her can of mace, her finger poised on the sprayer. *One. Two. Three!*

Shannon leapt into the room and flipped on the light. "Freeze!" She pointed her mace at the intruder, who hovered next to the worktable.

With his face covered by the ski mask, all Shannon could see of the intruder were his eyes—strangely familiar eyes. He snapped his head toward the window, as if he considered it a possible escape route. But Kate and Melanie appeared in view on the other side of the glass, both clad in black from head to toe, effectively blocking the window as an escape option.

Shannon heard Betty and Joyce join Deborah in the hall behind her. The intruder's eyes widened as their voices sounded.

"You're surrounded," Shannon said, pointing the mace at his face. "And the police are on their way. There's nowhere to escape."

The intruder's head swiveled from the door to the window and back again. Then he collapsed onto the floor and screamed in frustration.

Joyce marched into the room. "That doesn't sound like a man's voice." Her camouflage outfit—complete with pink leaves and rhinestone buttons—stuck out like a sore thumb next to Deborah and Betty, who followed close behind, both dressed entirely in black.

"Nooooo! I can't go back to jail!" the intruder wailed.

I know that voice. Shannon took a step forward. "Chloe?"

The intruder pulled off the mask and flung it across the room. Chloe's blue eyes glared at Shannon. "Now you've ruined everything!"

— 19 —

"Chloe Kitchener ... who would've guessed? I thought she'd straightened up her act." Joyce shook her head and took a sip of her coffee.

Seated around a table next to the window in Espresso Yourself, Melanie, Kate, and Betty all murmured sounds of agreement.

Kate turned to Shannon. "Has Chloe admitted to working with Fredo yet?"

Joyce snorted. "Working with him? How about *killing* him?"

Shannon shook her head. "Unfortunately, no. Grayson says she hasn't admitted to anything involving Fredo. She denies being his partner in crime, and she says she'd never kill anyone for any reason—Fredo included. They're checking into her alibis."

"She'll crack." Melanie slammed her petite fist on the table. "Give it time. They have ways of making people talk in the slammer."

All heads swiveled in her direction.

Melanie peered at the group from behind her glasses. "What?"

"You've been watching those crime shows Shannon likes, haven't you?" Betty fixed her with a knowing look.

"OK, yes, I admit it. She got me hooked." Melanie

grinned at Shannon. "But in all seriousness, I'm so glad this is over. I know how stressful these past few weeks have been for you—for all of us."

Shannon sighed. "Thanks. I couldn't have survived it without you all, and Deborah and Essie too." She glanced at Essie, who was busy fixing a drink behind the counter.

"Here's to us!" Joyce raised her mug, and the others joined in a group toast.

"May this autumn be far more peaceful than the summer's been," Kate added.

"Here! Here!" chorused the group.

Shannon took a sip of her iced coffee and glanced at the amazing group of women around the table. She felt truly blessed to have each one of them in her life—and to have the burglar behind bars. In a few days, she'd be finished with her repairs on the antique bag and could return it safe and sound to its rightful owner with a clear conscience.

*   *   *

On Friday evening, Shannon sat down in the study to finish Mrs. Reid's antique bag. Out of habit, she started to close the drapes. Then she changed her mind. *Chloe is in jail. I refuse to live in fear anymore.* She set out all her tools and the remaining beads needed to finish the design.

As before, holding the treasured item gave her a deep sense of satisfaction. It was nearly restored now, her workmanship virtually indistinguishable from that of the original artist. The silk thread and vintage beads blended perfectly with the rest of the stylized floral design. She eagerly got to work and became so immersed in the project that she jumped when Deborah's voice broke the silence.

"Thought you might be ready for a tea break."

Shannon looked up and smiled at her housekeeper, who stood poised in the doorway, holding a tea tray. "Oh, thank you. I am. Let's sit over there." She waved toward the chairs across the room from her worktable.

Deborah carried the tray with a teapot, two cups, and a small plate of brownies over to the piecrust table near the chairs. "How's it coming?"

Shannon stood and stretched. "I'm nearly finished. A few more beads, and then I can close up the lining. I think I'll be ready to call her tomorrow."

"Good. Even though the burglar's been caught, I suspect we'll both rest easier when it's gone." Deborah stirred her tea and set the spoon on the edge of her saucer. "I hate to bring up a difficult subject ... but I have to tell you, I really miss the twins."

Shannon sighed. "So do I."

"This big old house just seemed more alive while they were here."

"I agree." Shannon placed a brownie on her plate. "But don't worry, they'll be back. They've already started building fond memories of this place."

After they finished their tea, Shannon tried to go back to work on the bag, but Fredo Benson's creepy sketches of the Paisley mansion still nagged at her subconscious. Even though they'd caught Chloe in the act of trying to steal the bag, something still didn't fit.

It's over. Let it go.

A half hour later, she finally gave up on the bag and sat down at the computer, searching for the name "Fredo Benson" with other words like "forgery" and "prison." Her searches turned up very little, and then only things she already knew, like the fact that Fredo had been convicted two years earlier on a forgery count. No details were given.

She felt the twins' absence keenly when she went up to her bedroom a couple of hours later. With Deborah in her room on the first floor, Shannon was alone upstairs, and her steps in the carpeted hallway whispered, though she felt they ought to echo in hollowness. She paused by Alec's door and then Lara's, gazing in at their empty rooms. Tears sprang into her eyes when she noticed the plush bear Lara had left among the colorful cushions on her bed. Shannon moved on before she had a chance to go all teary.

She did not want to go into the turret room, but she didn't feel comfortable leaving Mrs. Reid's bag anywhere else—even though Chloe had been caught. *Why am I feeling this way? Is paranoia a side effect of empty-nest syndrome?* She made the foray quickly and hid the bag securely in its niche.

Heading back to the opulent master suite, she reflected on Essie's comment about Chloe having a crush on Fredo. *Did she kill him out of jealousy? Were they truly partners in crime?*

When she finally climbed into her carved teak bed and set aside the embroidered decorative pillows, she turned off the lamp, closed her eyes, and forced herself to banish all thoughts of Chloe and Fredo from her mind. She spent a few minutes in drowsy prayer and drifted off into sweet slumber.

* * *

Shannon wasn't sure what woke her. *At least it's not the security alarm—thank heaven!* She raised her head off the pillow and cocked an ear toward the door. When she'd decided it was only a "house noise," it came again—a muffled thump followed by a soft, grating sound, like something being slid or dragged.

Sitting up, she reached for the robe she'd left draped over the footboard. It was probably Deborah rambling about in the kitchen, but she needed to be sure. A glance at the clock told her it was two in the morning.

She tiptoed to the door, turned the knob, and eased it open, relieved that it didn't squeak. As quietly as possible, she inched along the darkened hall toward the stairway landing. She was halfway there when a soft light appeared in the foyer below. Barely able to breathe, she eased closer to the railing. The light moved about, playing over the walls and floor.

It wasn't a lamp. A dark figure slipped from behind the silhouette of the huge rearing horse statue and moved along one wall of the foyer, the beam of light preceding it, to a niche in the wall that held a small bronze of a frolicking child. The light paused near the bronze, and Shannon heard small noises. Was the person below trying to steal the statue? Or was he looking for something else in the niche? Either way, it couldn't be Deborah down there.

Shannon's heart beat double-time. *How can this be happening again? Surely Grayson would've told me if they'd released Chloe.* The realization hit her then—Chloe had been telling the truth. She wasn't responsible for the previous break-ins, and she probably had nothing to do with

Fredo's death. *This nightmare still isn't over. We caught the wrong burglar.*

Shannon shivered and held her breath. The last thing she wanted to do was to give away her presence. She stepped back with supreme caution. When she was confident that the intruder's beam couldn't find her if he shone the light up toward the landing, she turned and fled along the hall.

She darted into her bedroom and closed the door all but a couple of inches. Then she put her ear close to the crack and listened.

Nothing.

She tiptoed to the bedside table and felt for her cordless phone. She carried it into her bathroom and called 911.

"Nine-one-one. What is your emergency?"

"There's a burglar in my house. Please hurry."

Shannon gave her name and confirmed the address.

"We'll have someone there right away," the dispatcher said. "Can you get out of the house?"

"I don't think so. I'm upstairs, and the intruder is downstairs near the front door."

"Did you confront him?"

"No."

"Does he know you're in the house?"

"I'm not sure." Shannon exhaled a shaky breath. "I suspect he does."

"Do you think he came in the front door?"

"I don't really know. My house has a full alarm system, but it didn't go off. I don't understand it."

"Officers are on the way," the dispatcher said. "Is there anyone else in the house?"

"Yes, my housekeeper. Her bedroom is downstairs."

Thinking of Deborah made Shannon's pulse skyrocket. *Had she heard the intruder? Was she huddled in her bathroom again, praying he wouldn't find her?*

"Hold on," Shannon said into the phone. The dispatcher launched into a "stay on the line" lecture, but Shannon shoved the phone into the pocket of her housecoat and tip-toed out into her bedroom. At the hall door, she listened for several seconds and heard a soft thump from the direction of the staircase.

Retreating a few steps into her room, she put the phone to her ear. The dispatcher was saying, "Mrs. McClain? Are you there?"

"I need to warn my housekeeper," she whispered.

"Stay where you know you're safe, ma'am," the dispatcher said firmly.

Shannon knew that was sound advice, but she couldn't bear to think of Deborah all alone downstairs with the thief. She might not even know the house had been invaded again, but if she did, she'd be terrified. The last incident had shaken Deborah badly. Shannon couldn't let her go through it again, cowering in her room alone.

Shannon considered her options. If the intruder went into her study to search it, maybe she could slip across the foyer to the dining room doorway and through that room to the kitchen. She could join Deborah in her quarters, and they could wait for the police together. It seemed worth the risk to Shannon.

Assuring herself that she absolutely would not take a chance if the burglar was still in the foyer, she told the dispatcher, "I'll be back," and laid the phone on the night-stand. If she took it with her, the burglar might hear the dispatcher talking, but she didn't want to break the connection completely. She could faintly hear the dispatcher's protests as she felt for the large flashlight she kept in the bottom of her nightstand. *If need be, I'll use it as a club. Oh, how I wish the Purls were here with me now!*

She slid into the hall once more, listened, and when she heard nothing, crept toward the landing to look over the railing.

Downstairs, the faint glow of a flashlight shone from the hallway that led to her study. Shannon inched down the steps, bending low at the waist. If his light grew brighter, she'd duck down and hope he couldn't see her. Her heart thudded in her ears as she climbed down another step, her gaze riveted on the glimmer of light coming from the hallway.

Halfway down the steps, she reached the point where the staircase curved enough so that she could see a short distance into the hall. Her breath caught, and she froze. The intruder wasn't on his way into the study after all. He stood directly in front of the wall case that held the antique dueling pistols that Alec admired.

Shannon's heart sank. *If I continue down into the foyer, he'll see me. How am I going to get to Deborah?*

— 20 —

Shannon felt certain the intruder was a man, though his back was to her. Trapped on the staircase, she shrank back from the railing, keeping her gaze on the burglar. The best plan she could come up with was to sneak back up the stairs and wait up there for the police.

At least I know the thief isn't headed toward Deborah's room.

To her chagrin, she saw the man turn slightly as he opened the glass case. *He's going to steal the pistols!*

Trying to stop him would be foolhardy in the extreme. She'd have to depend on Chief Grayson and his men to recover the pistols and anything else the thief had already taken. Shannon's face heated, and she clenched her fist around the darkened flashlight. If the thief had come for Mrs. Reid's bag, he'd clearly changed his agenda. It appeared he intended to take whatever caught his eye.

Shannon glanced at the umbrella stand near the bottom of the stairs on her right. It held a couple of umbrellas and a carved wooden walking stick. If the burglar attacked her, the walking stick would be a much better weapon than the flashlight and would allow Shannon to strike from a greater distance. She debated for a moment over whether to bend down and reach between the balusters to grip the end of it, or to flee up the stairs. Either way, he might hear her, and the top end of the stick was only inches from her grasp.

She set down the flashlight on the step above her, held on to the railing with one hand, and leaned down as far as she could. Her fingers closed on the top of the walking stick. Relieved, she gently pulled it up.

The bottom end of the stick had almost cleared the top of the stand when a muscle in Shannon's neck knotted, causing the stick to clack against the side of the umbrella stand, making the tiniest of sounds. She flinched, and the resulting clang of stick against stand sounded to her as loud as someone dropping a china dish.

Adrenaline rushed through her body, and she looked toward the hallway. The dark-clothed man turned toward her, pistol in hand, and slowly pulled back the hammer.

Surely, it's not loaded! Shannon yanked the walking stick toward her, between the balusters.

An explosion roared, echoing off the high ceiling and walls of the foyer. At the same time, a flash of fiery light flickered near his hand, and something thunked into the wall above the bottom step.

Shannon couldn't move. Despite the immediate danger to herself, all she could think was that Alec could have been killed if he'd messed with the pistol. Her ears began to ring, and she watched as the burglar lowered the pistol and raised his flashlight, shining the beam directly into her eyes.

He took a step toward her.

Shannon clutched the end of the walking stick. "Don't come any closer!"

In the shadows beyond him, near the dining room door, she noticed a furtive movement. Her throat constricted. *Are there two of them?* In an instant, she took in the light-colored, flowing garment.

Deborah!

The intruder heard the housekeeper's soft footsteps and whirled, shining his flashlight on her, catching her stretched up to her full height with her arms raised. She held a rolling pin over her head. Shannon gripped the walking stick and dashed down the last few steps. At the same moment, the man shoved Deborah into the wall. She thumped against it and slid to the floor.

Shannon was upon him, and she didn't care how badly she hurt him. She brought the walking stick down as hard as she could on the back of his head and shoulders. The man sank to his knees, dropping the pistol. His flashlight rolled across the floor, sending crazy shadows dancing across the walls and ceiling. Shannon stood over him and raised the stick again, ready to deliver another blow, though her knees shook violently. The burglar swayed a little and started to put his right hand up to his head, then toppled over on the marble floor.

The chandelier flashed into its blazing splendor. Deborah had managed to get to the switch and flip it on, flooding the foyer with glorious, revealing light. The intruder's form lay crumpled at Shannon's feet.

The ringing in her ears finally began to recede, and all at once she heard sirens screaming. Relief flooded through her.

She looked over at Deborah. At the same instant, they both dashed for the front door. Deborah attacked the deadbolt, and Shannon turned to the alarm keypad. To her surprise, its display panel was blank.

Deborah had the door open before Shannon could pull her thoughts together. Chief Grayson and Officer Doan ran in, their weapons drawn.

"He's over there!" Shannon pointed to where the burglar struggled to rise.

He managed to get to his knees, but Officer Doan shoved him back down.

"Police! Stay down and put your hands behind your back!"

Shannon drew a deep breath. The walking stick was still in her hand, clutched in a grip so tight her knuckles were white. She slowly lowered it and let the tip rest on the floor. Grayson's gaze darted from her to Deborah.

"Everyone all right?"

"Yes," Shannon said. "Shocked, but fine."

Deborah nodded.

A satisfying *click* sounded as Officer Doan secured the burglar with handcuffs.

"Only one suspect?" Grayson asked.

"Yes," Shannon said. "I saw him from up there." She pointed to the landing above. "I only saw one person and one light."

"He's all I saw too." Deborah tightened the belt on her robe. "I wouldn't have come out, but I heard a shot, and I was afraid someone had hurt Shannon."

A little laugh burbled up in Shannon's chest. "It was one of the old dueling pistols, of all things. I had no idea they were loaded, or that they could even fire."

"Me either." Deborah stared wide-eyed at the antique walnut, steel, and brass weapon that lay on the floor at the base of the statue. "I can't believe Mrs. Paisley didn't have them checked."

Shannon looked at the gun, all traces of laughter gone from her face. "Alec asked me about the guns, but I told him not to touch them."

"Good thing," Deborah said darkly.

"I was afraid he'd shoot again," Shannon said, looking toward the subdued prisoner. "And when he pushed Deborah—well, I hit him with this." She held the tall walking stick out, and Grayson took it, eyeing it gravely.

"Those old pistols are single-shots," he said, "but he might have had a gun of his own."

"Yes, or taken out the other dueling pistol." Shannon walked over to Deborah and put her arms around her. "Thank you for helping me, dear friend. If you hadn't come out here, who knows what would have happened?"

They held each other for a moment, and then Deborah stepped back and wiped her eyes with her bathrobe sleeve. She looked at Grayson and swallowed hard. "If you don't mind, I think I'll go into the kitchen and sit down for a minute. And then I'll make some coffee for everyone."

"You don't need to do that for us," Grayson said. "Just sit and relax. We'll come in and get your statement after we're done here."

Deborah nodded and shuffled toward the kitchen, her slippers scuffing on the marble floor.

After Officer Doan read the man his rights, Grayson walked over to stand beside the patrolman.

"Here's his ID." Officer Doan handed Grayson a wallet.

The chief opened it and looked inside, frowning as he studied the driver's license. Shannon edged closer, but not so near that Grayson would bark at her.

"All right, Mr. Tuttle, what's the story?" Grayson said gruffly.

Shannon eyed the man on the floor. *This must be Lois Reid's cousin, Warren Tuttle.*

Warren remained silent.

"Get him up," Grayson told the officer.

Officer Doan hauled the prisoner to his feet.

"We know this isn't the first time you've been in here." Grayson narrowed his eyes at the man. "This time, you cut the wires on the alarm system. But you still didn't find what you were looking for, did you?"

Warren met the chief's hard gaze. "I didn't take anything."

"Oh yeah? What do you call that?" Grayson pointed at the pistol on the floor.

"I didn't steal it. And I didn't know it was loaded either. That crazy woman scared me, I jumped, and it went off— took ten years off my life when the thing fired."

Grayson smirked. "Convenient story, but I'm not buying it. You had to cock it first. We'll take a few more years off your life and let you think about it in jail."

Outside, another siren wailed, and blue light flashed across the walls as an SUV pulled into the circle drive.

"That's Brownley," Officer Doan said.

Grayson handed him the wallet. "Get Mr. Tuttle out of here."

Officer Doan herded his prisoner out the front door. Shannon stood in the doorway, watching as he put the man into the backseat of Officer Brownley's vehicle.

She turned to Grayson. "Something told me Chloe wasn't the root cause of this mess. Do you think it's possible they were working together?"

Grayson shook his head. "Her alibis for the previous break-in at your store and for Fredo's time of death are airtight.

I think she was simply doing what Chloe does best the night you caught her here—she was being opportunistic."

"I hope Warren confesses so we can finally put this behind us once and for all."

"We'll get it out of him, don't worry," Grayson said. "We already know about his desire to buy the antique bag—and the pin you found inside it—from his cousin, Lois Reid."

"And how he assaulted her when she refused to sell them."

"Mm-hm. That's a big advantage for us," Grayson said. "Last week, I asked the Multnomah County sheriff's office to question him, since he lives over there, but he kept dodging them, and they hadn't caught up to him yet. Keep this to yourself if you would. We'll contact Mrs. Reid too, of course."

Shannon glanced at the alarm keypad on the wall by the front door. "You said Warren cut the wires on the alarm?"

"I haven't looked, but that's my guess. The alarm is what got him in trouble last time and cut short his search, so he decided to disable it. I'll have Michael come take a look at it to see exactly how Tuttle did it. You can't just cut a wire and disable the whole system without triggering a signal to the security company. This guy must have done his homework. You should notify the company and have them send a repairman out as soon as possible."

Shannon nodded. "How can we be sure it was Warren Tuttle the other times?"

"We'll get all of that from him, sooner or later." Grayson sighed. "I'm sorry it took us so long to catch him, and that you and Deborah were endangered tonight."

Shannon gave a little laugh that sounded almost like a

sob. "I'm just glad you and Officer Doan got here so quickly." Her gaze focused on the wall near the stairs. The hole in the sheetrock was only about a half inch wide, but it grimly reminded her of the moment when the old weapon had roared. "That's where the pistol bullet hit."

Grayson went up the first two steps and examined the wall closely. "I'll have my men come back in the morning and see if they can get the ball out. Don't touch it until they're finished—you can have it repaired afterward. Oh, and I'll take that pistol with me. You'll get it back eventually, of course."

"Do you want to take its mate?" Shannon pointed toward the hallway. "It's still there in the case."

"No, but I'll check it and see if it's loaded. No sense leaving weapons lying around for criminals to use against you."

"I'd be grateful," Shannon said. "I still can't believe it was sitting there ready to fire all this time."

Officer Doan entered through the dining room door. "He broke in through the back of the house again, Chief—same door he used before, only this time, no alarm."

Grayson nodded. "I figured. You didn't find any wire cutters on Tuttle, did you?"

"No, but I spotted his car. There's a dark-colored Chevy parked out behind the summer house, on the access road to the lake. I checked the license plate on the computer, and it's Tuttle's car."

"Good work," Grayson said.

Shannon smiled at them. "I'm going to leave you gentlemen to do what you do so well and go see how Deborah is coping with all of this. After all she's had to endure recently, if she resigns on the spot, I won't be surprised."

"She was making coffee when I came through the kitchen," Officer Doan said.

"If you'd like some, feel free." Shannon nodded at Grayson and headed to the kitchen.

She found Deborah bustling about, still in her robe and slippers. She'd set out four mugs, spoons, napkins, the sugar bowl, and flavored creamers.

"Think they'd like some sugar cookies?"

"I don't know," Shannon said, "but I'd love one."

Deborah set a plastic container on the counter and opened it. "They can help themselves." She turned and met Shannon's gaze. "It didn't really hit me that the man fired a gun at you until I came out here and set to work. I started shaking so bad, I almost dropped the coffeepot."

Shannon walked over and gave her a squeeze. "He shoved you pretty hard too. Are you sure you're all right?"

"Oh, yes, I'm fine."

The teakettle whistled, and Shannon jumped. "You're making tea *and* coffee?"

Deborah turned off the burner and lifted the teakettle off. "Yes, I am. Those men can drink all the strong coffee they want in the middle of the night. I know you better, and I'm brewing us some chamomile tea."

"Brilliant choice." Shannon took a cookie and a napkin from the counter and sat down at the table. A minute later, Deborah joined her with their mugs of tea.

"Are you going to tell the kids about Chloe or Warren or any part of what's gone on this week since they left?" Deborah asked.

"I'll have to. At least now I can tell them with confidence

that the thief is in custody."

An hour later, after Deborah and Shannon had given their official statements, Grayson and his men left, taking the pistol that had been fired. As promised, he'd checked the second pistol and had unloaded it, removing both cap and ball.

When Shannon retired to her bedroom, she turned off her alarm clock. The next morning, Essie was scheduled to open the store, and after all Shannon had endured, a little extra sleep couldn't hurt. Though she feared she wouldn't be able to stop her mind from racing, the knowledge that the *real* thief had been apprehended allowed her to fall asleep easily.

She awoke to Deborah tapping on her door. "Shannon?"

"Yes?" Shannon sat up, blinking at the brightly lit room. She squinted at the clock. The display showed ten minutes past eight.

Deborah cracked the door open. "Sorry to bother you, but Michael is downstairs. I gave him coffee and said I'd check to see if you were awake."

Shannon laughed. "Well, I am now. Thanks."

"I figured you wouldn't want me to send him away." Deborah winked.

"Oh, you did?" Shannon arched her eyebrows at her friend. "Well, you figured right." She threw back the covers and sat up. "I need to call Essie and make sure she can open the store. Please tell him I'll be down in five minutes." She was being optimistic, but she managed to make herself presentable in not much more time than that.

She found Michael seated at the kitchen table with Deborah. A plate of scrambled eggs and whole wheat toast sat in front of him.

He smiled and stood as soon as he caught sight of her. "Good morning."

"Same to you." Shannon smoothed her haphazard ponytail and returned his smile.

"Deborah talked me into breakfast," he said.

"No sense waiting with an empty stomach." Deborah got up and carried her plate to the sink. "I've got plenty of eggs. I can do sausage too, if you want it."

"No thanks." Shannon took her seat. "Eggs and toast is fine, and some tea if—"

"If, nothing," Deborah said. "I've got it all ready." She poured it from the teapot on the counter and had a steaming cup of tea in front of Shannon in seconds.

"I'm spoiled, I admit it." Shannon smiled at Michael. "I take it you heard about last night."

"From Grayson, yes. Deborah filled me in on more of the details. I'd ask if you're all right, but it's obvious you're doing fine."

Shannon nodded. "I'll be better once we know for certain who was behind each break-in and who killed Fredo."

"Grayson says Tuttle talked."

"Really? I didn't think he would. Last night he was very quiet." Shannon sipped her tea. "Anything I want to know?"

"It seems this Tuttle fellow knew a friend of Fredo Benson's from his time in prison. You know he'd expected to inherit something that went to his cousin."

"Yes—Mrs. Reid, my client. Her grandmother changed her will."

"That's right. She cut Tuttle out when he went to jail a few years ago. Well, Tuttle tried to get the antique bag from his cousin. She wouldn't give it up, as you're aware. Then Tuttle went back to jail on an unrelated assault charge. That's when he heard about Fredo Benson. After he was released, he tried to talk to his cousin again. He found out she'd taken the bag to you to be repaired. Tuttle decided an artist with a criminal bent could come in handy."

"You mean Fredo came and rented the loft from me just to try to get at Lois Reid's bag?"

"Apparently so."

"Then he's been stalking me—my house—for as long as I've had the bag." She thought for a moment. "Months!"

"Looks that way. Tuttle paid him to look around your store to see if he could get his hands on it. When that failed to produce results, he started snooping around your house."

Shannon nodded. "That explains why he took pictures in here. He wasn't sloppy though—we were probably the sloppy ones. Often times we forgot to set the alarm. And I never knew he'd been inside until I saw the painting and sketches he'd made from the photos."

"It seems Tuttle decided Benson wasn't aggressive enough. He wanted Benson to really tear this place apart and find that bag. He admits putting the butterfly pin in it well before his grandmother died. He was looking for a double payoff, thinking he'd inherit the bag. He and Benson had a big argument over it. Tuttle said Benson was determined not to go back to jail."

"Good for him!" Shannon stared at Michael for a moment. "Oh. Is that how Fredo died?"

"I'm afraid so. Tuttle hit him with a wrench and killed him. Then he went to your store and ransacked your office, trying to find the bag himself. He couldn't open the safe, and he couldn't move it far by himself either. He had to flee before the police arrived. For some reason, after that, he seemed to know it was in your house and concentrated on that instead of the store."

Shannon shivered. "He may have seen me working on it through the window."

"That might explain why he tossed your study first."

"Yeah, he went for that and my bedroom. This last time, it seemed he might be considering stealing a few other things. I suspect he planned to compensate himself for his trouble if he couldn't find the bag."

"I saw that antique pistol he fired off." Michael's voice wavered slightly. "You could've been killed last night, Shannon."

She held his concerned gaze. "I know." After a moment, she took a sip of tea and tried to lighten the mood. "You can bet I won't leave loaded guns hanging on my walls in the future. If someone wants to kill me, I'm going to make them work a little harder at it."

A hint of a smile tugged at the corners of Michael's lips. "I thought I'd take a look at your alarms while I'm here."

"Would you?" Shannon glanced at her watch. "I told Essie I'd be in around ten, so there's plenty of time."

"Finish your breakfast," Michael said, rising. "I'll go take a look at things, and then we'll call the security company."

"Do you think I need a better system?" Shannon asked.

Michael shook his head. "Tuttle had to know what he was doing to disconnect it without setting off the alarm. Not many people have that kind of knowledge. Still, a few more deadbolts might not be a bad idea. If a thief is determined, there's not much that will stop him, as you've seen. But you can slow him down a lot."

"Thank you."

He smiled, and her pulse surged. "I'm just glad you and Deborah are all right." He went out the back door whistling.

*   *   *

Later that afternoon, Alec called her cellphone.

Shannon smiled as she answered, "Hello, love."

"Hey, Mum. We're at a place called Bridal Veil Falls. You'd love it! It's the biggest waterfall I've ever seen. A real stunner!"

"It sounds gorgeous."

"Oop, hold on. Lara's up on the bridge with a friend of hers, and I'm supposed to take a picture. They're waving at me." A moment later, Alec returned. "All set. How are things at home?"

"Good," Shannon said. "You'll be happy to know that Fredo Benson's murderer is in jail."

"I'll say! Is he the same fellow who broke into the house?"

"Yes and no." Shannon filled him in on everything that had happened since they'd left.

"Wait 'til I tell Lara," he said. "She was really worried about you and Deborah."

Shannon smiled to herself. *Lara wasn't the one who called Michael and asked him to check up on me.*

"We want to come home and visit next weekend," Alec said. "Can you come pick us up on Friday afternoon?"

"I sure can. You have fun on the rest of your trip, and send me a couple of photos, you hear?"

"Will do. Love you, Mum."

Shannon hung up with a smile on her face. She hoped all would be peaceful as they headed into autumn—she'd had enough excitement for a good, long while.

Learn more about Annie's fiction books at

AnniesFiction.com

- Access your e-books
- Discover exciting new series
- Read sample chapters
- Watch video book trailers
- Share your feedback

We've designed the Annie's Fiction website especially for you!

Plus, manage your account online!

- Check your account status
- Make payments online
- Update your address

Visit us at AnniesFiction.com

Turn the page for an exclusive preview
of the next mystery in the
Creative Woman Mysteries series.

Dog Gone Shame

COMING SOON!

1

"**W**ho knew choosing a champion dog involved so much work?" Shannon McClain brushed her unruly red curls off her face and settled the last folding chair in place inside the tent set up in Main Street Park in downtown Apple Grove.

She stood back to admire her work while her good friend and the owner of Ultimutt Grooming, Kate Ellis, knelt on the tent's earthen floor, attaching row numbers to the chairs. Tomorrow morning, owners would prance their purebred dogs around the center ring in hopes of winning Best in Show in the first Apple Grove Dog Show and Pet Fair, an event that organizers hoped would turn into an annual affair.

A contented sigh slipped from Shannon's mouth as she strolled across the tent to Kate. Shannon loved helping her knitting group, the Purls of Hope, raise money for local charities. This time around, they were raising funds for the local animal shelter. Not that Shannon was familiar with animals—far from it—but Kate possessed ample knowledge to make the show a success.

As Shannon approached her friend, Kate's head popped up. "All finished?"

Shannon nodded. "And it's only eight o'clock."

"It can't be eight!" Kate's eyes filled with panic as her gaze flew to her watch. "Oh, no, it *is* eight. I'm in big trouble. I was supposed to walk Scarlet thirty minutes ago."

She leapt to her feet. As she did, her foot caught on a

chair, collapsing the frame and thrusting it into a neighboring chair.

Shannon grabbed Kate's arm to steady her before she tumbled to the ground too. Tears formed in Kate's large brown eyes.

"Hey." Shannon smiled at her flustered friend. "Are you OK?"

Kate shook her head. "Millicent Downing has lectured me about being late for Scarlet's walk in the past. She says a champion dog like Scarlet needs to be kept on a strict schedule. Millicent's going to be livid when she finds out I didn't get to Scarlet on time." Kate shoved the cardboard numbers into Shannon's hands. "I need to go."

"I thought you told me Millicent left early this morning for her spa weekend." Shannon tapped the cards' edges to straighten them.

"She did."

"Then she won't know if you're a little bit late."

"Hah! Millicent knows everything. No doubt she'll call me on the carpet for it when she returns. What's worse, if she complains to other pet owners in town, it will cost me a lot of business." Kate chewed on her bottom lip, removing the last of her berry lip gloss. "I have to get over there right away."

"Do you want me to go with you?"

"No. You keep working on setup. I'll be fine." Kate grabbed her backpack from the large metal cart once filled with chairs and slipped a strap over her shoulder. "I'll be back in an hour, tops." She marched out of the tent, her long ponytail swinging.

Shannon straightened the chairs, then attached the

remaining aisle numbers. After a quick check to ensure the tent was ready for the morning, she pushed the cart outside for storage. The rubber wheels squeaked as she hurried through Main Street Park. Across the street, the Paisley Craft Market & Artist Lofts—the business she'd inherited from her grandmother, Victoria Paisley—was the only building in a line of many quaint shops where lights burned inside.

Her shop wasn't open for business, but work awaited the remaining members of the Purls inside before they could head home for the night. Three members of the group—Melanie, Betty and Joyce—finished setting up tables nearby under tall trees. The leaves above them whispered in the strong ocean breeze that brought with it a hint of cooler fall temperatures.

As she parked the cart in a small storage area near the group, a couple who looked to be in their sixties strolled by, holding hands. As Shannon watched the man gaze down at his companion with affection, it wasn't the usual bitter longing that settled over her, but a strange inner peace instead. Peace she'd longed for since the death of her husband John more than three years earlier. Maybe she'd finally turned the corner and was ready to move on and fully embrace life again. If her dear friend Coleen Douglas were with her instead of in Scotland, she'd sing out a hearty "Halleluiah!" and say it was about time—as would the Purls who glanced down the path at the sound of her footsteps.

Shannon smiled at her friends. Betty Russo, the extremely social owner of The Apple Grove Inn, held a plastic tablecloth in her capable hands. Next to her stood Joyce Buchanan, whose platinum bob swung as she settled a cloth over a long table.

Melanie Burkhart finished a sign and clicked the cap on her marker, her hair now falling in shoulder-length waves after her recent battle with breast cancer. They, along with Shannon and Kate, formed the small group of women who gathered each week at the craft market to knit and socialize.

"We saw Kate race out of here. Is anything wrong?" Betty spread the cloth over one of the tables set up for the next day's vendors.

Shannon took a corner of the cloth and helped press it in place. "She lost track of time and was late for walking Millicent Downing's dog. Kate thinks she'll be in trouble with Millicent when she finds out Scarlet's walk was thirty minutes overdue."

"She has plenty to worry about, if you ask me." Joyce slipped shiny clips on the table edges to keep the breeze from sending the cloth airborne. "Millicent has quite the reputation for being demanding."

"I'll say. Just the other day, she yelled at Elaina at The Flower Pot." Melanie heard plenty of gossip while working at her part-time jobs at The Flower Pot and Shannon's craft market. "Millicent said the flower arrangement she'd purchased didn't last as long as she expected. Even though she'd gotten her money's worth, Elaina gave her a full refund to keep her from bad-mouthing her business all over town."

Shannon hated to hear one of her fellow business owners had been mistreated. "I thought Millicent was wealthy. Is she hard up for money?"

Joyce snorted. "Not at all. Her husband died a few years ago. That's when she moved to Apple Grove and bought the priciest house on the market."

"She's not motivated by money then?" Shannon asked.

"No." Melanie ripped open another package. "She's motivated by mean."

"What a thing to say, Mel," Joyce chided her.

Melanie settled her hands on her hips. "Well she *is* mean."

"But you don't have to say it." Joyce's lips narrowed into a flat line of disapproval.

"You're right. I'm sorry," Melanie said contritely. "I don't mean to speak ill of her, but I get tired of the Millicents of the world getting their way by keeping decent, hardworking people like Kate and Elaina under their thumb."

"Maybe we should change the subject," Betty suggested in her usual peacemaking tone.

Shannon couldn't agree more. "Where do we stand with the show's preparations?"

Betty ran her hands over a bright blue cloth, smoothing out wrinkles in the plastic. "Once we finish the tables, we need to price our sweaters, and then we can call it a night."

The Purls had been knitting adorable doggie sweaters to donate to the cause for a month or so. They'd completed enough sweaters to fill five large boxes now stored inside the craft market. Wanting to carry on her grandmother's charitable ways, Shannon had provided the yarn and offered to store the sweaters at her shop.

"Then let's finish the tables and head over to the craft market so we can get home at a decent hour tonight." Betty stifled a yawn. As the oldest of the group, she often tired first, but Shannon suspected she really wanted to get home and dive into one of her favorite Jane Austen novels.

When they'd settled the last tablecloth in place and collected the plastic wrappers, Melanie slipped her arm around Joyce's shoulder. She led the group through the park where swaying Oregon pines towered over more wooden picnic tables. Miniature white lights twinkled from the trees and lit the park with a romantic hue.

At the curb, Shannon stopped to open the power box and flip the switch. The lights in the trees and the large white tent darkened, making the brightly lit parking lot stand out.

Joyce tipped her head at the many motor homes and trailers parked in the lot. "We have a good turnout for the show already. I hope this place will be packed tomorrow."

Melanie smiled at Betty. "Your idea to rent spaces in the lot for the dog owners to camp out was pure genius. The fees will raise a substantial amount of money."

As the owner of The Apple Grove Inn, Betty had already offered to donate half of her proceeds for the weekend. Then she took it a step further to obtain permits needed for owners to camp in the public parking lot.

"I don't know about genius," Betty laughed, "but it seemed like a logical idea."

"Well, I still say you're a genius," Melanie added. "I don't have any of the business savvy you possess. Makes sense that I'm the only one in the group who doesn't own a shop."

"I'm glad you don't own anything." Joyce smiled at Melanie. "You can give all of us advice from a customer's perspective."

Melanie rubbed her tummy and grinned. "I'm more than happy to give you advice about your baking anytime you need it."

"Then let's get going. I have a box of Joyce's famous cupcakes at the shop," Shannon said. The thought of biting into one of Joyce's Pink Sprinkle's Bakery creations made her mouth water. She crossed the street and unlocked the front door to the Paisley Craft Market & Artist Lofts. The first floor of the shop boasted supplies for every type of craft the locals could want to engage in, while the second floor held loft studios rented to artists. Her friends strolled to the coffee shop's sitting area, where the Purls met for their weekly knitting sessions. Store manager Essie Engleman had set out boxes of sweaters and a stack of blank price tags before closing for the night.

"Anyone want coffee or tea with their cupcakes?" Shannon tipped her head at the long coffee bar in Espresso Yourself.

"Coffee, please ..." Betty sank into one of the buttery-soft leather chairs and rubbed her arthritis-riddled knee. "... if you wouldn't mind getting it for me."

"I'll help you," Joyce offered. "Did you want anything, Mel?"

Melanie shook her head and pulled a pile of tiny red sweaters out of a box.

Shannon stepped behind the counter, running her hand along the stone top. She still found it hard to believe she'd been so blessed by not only inheriting the craft market and her home, Paisley mansion, but also seeing her dreams of adding a cozy coffee shop come to fruition. She pumped steaming black coffee into a mug for Joyce and put it on a tray.

Betty added sugar and cream, then nodded toward the window. "Isn't that Michael Stone's car?"

Shannon spun in time to see Michael unfold his long, lean body from his vehicle. He wore dark jeans and a yellow polo shirt that made his dark hair look jet-black under the streetlight. He stopped on the sidewalk and peered into the window before offering Shannon a tentative wave.

"Looks like someone's here to see you." Joyce gave Shannon a nudge toward the door.

"You don't know that."

"It's pretty obvious with the way he's staring at you."

Joyce was right. He'd fixed his cobalt blue eyes on Shannon, and she was powerless to look away. The Purls often teased her that Michael was interested in her romantically, but he hadn't said a word to make her believe that was true. Shannon suspected the Purls only wanted to play matchmaker. Michael had lost his wife ten years earlier when a criminal had shot her in retaliation for a drug bust. No longer a police detective, Michael now co-owned Stone & McCrary Security Consultants. He'd helped Shannon solve a few local crimes since her arrival in town—and he'd saved her life. They'd gotten to know each other quite well. As friends. Never had they talked about more.

Betty pointedly cleared her throat.

Shannon caught herself staring and felt the heat of a blush rise over her cheeks. "I'll go see what he wants."

Hoping to tame wild curls that the ocean humidity often sent awry, she ran a hand over her fiery red hair and stepped outside.

Michael walked toward her, his confident stride unusually tentative. "You're working late."

"We still have a lot left to do for tomorrow's show." Trying to get a read on his reason for being there at such an odd hour, she watched him for a moment. If he had a purpose for his visit, he hid it well. "Did you need something, Michael?"

He opened his mouth and started to form a word, then clamped his lips shut. Not being an indecisive man, his action surprised Shannon. She waited without speaking to see what he'd do next.

"I was wondering," he finally said. "Would ..." His voice drifted off, and he toed his shoe at a sidewalk crack.

Fearing he had bad news to share, Shannon stepped forward and touched his arm. "What is it?"

He eyed her for a long moment then shook his head. "Never mind. It's nothing."

"But you—"

"Have to get going," he interrupted. "Will I see you here tomorrow?"

Confused by his behavior, she slowly nodded. "I'll be working from sunup to sundown."

"That'll be a long day."

She shrugged. "It's for a good cause."

"I'll be in town tomorrow. Is there anything I can do to help?"

"We have everything covered, but if something comes up, I'll give you a call."

"OK, see you later."

Bewildered, Shannon watched him walk away.

He was halfway to his car when he stopped abruptly and spun. "I have this thing for work," he blurted. "A party we hold every year for our associates to say thank you for their hard work. Anyway, it can be awkward going alone to events like this, and I thought maybe you'd like to accompany me this year."

"Accompany you?" Shannon replied, stunned by the unexpected turn the conversation had taken.

"Yeah … you know … go with me." A timid tenor filled his voice. He slowly strode toward her until he stood less than a foot away.

"Like on a …" She flapped her hands nervously in the air, searching for the word her mind *refused* to provide.

He took a step back. "If you'd rather not go, I understand."

She shook her head. "No, no … I mean, yes, I'd like to go."

"Yes?"

"*Yes.*" She nodded for emphasis and willed her arms to stop fluttering about like the wings of a crazy chicken.

"Great. That's just great." He started backing toward his car, his expression a mixture of happiness and horror.

Shannon's mind raced. *What if his partner pressured him to bring someone along, and he asked me out of duty, all the while hoping I'd say no?*

"You're sure you want me to go?" she asked.

"Yes, of course." The corners of his mouth lifted slightly. "That is, if you want to."

"I do," she answered without thinking. "When is this event, anyway?"

"Saturday at seven."

Shannon gulped. "Saturday—two days from now?"

"Yes, is that problem?" he asked.

"No, not at all."

"It's too short notice, isn't it?" He pulled a hand through his hair. "I shouldn't have waited so long. I didn't think of it until the other day, and I figured we'd run into each other sooner. We can forget about it." With hands up as if in surrender, Michael began backing toward his car again.

She shot out a hand. "No, wait. I want to go."

"You do? Honestly?"

She did. She really did. More than she thought she'd want to. "Yes."

"OK then, I'll see you Saturday." With a boyish grin on his face, he turned to leave.

"I thought you were going to attend the show tomorrow?"

"Right," he said quickly. "I'll see you tomorrow then." He hurried to his car, and, too stunned to move, she waited as he climbed in.

She closed her eyes for a moment, trying to imagine a night out with Michael, but shock wouldn't let her visualize it. *I'm going out with Michael. Michael! On a date. But is it really a date, or one of those events where everyone is obliged to bring someone with them to even out the numbers? Och! I forgot to ask where we're going.*

Her cellphone chimed from her pocket, startling her. She dug it out, not at all surprised to see Kate's icon on the screen.

"Did you change your mind and want me to walk Scarlet with you?" Shannon asked, relieved to have a distraction.

Kate started sobbing and mumbled something Shannon couldn't understand.

Unease settled in Shannon's heart. "What happened? Was Millicent home? Did she fire you?"

"She ... she's here." A strangled cry tore from Kate.

Anger over the thought of Millicent mistreating her friend had Shannon fisting her free hand. "Do you need me come over there and talk to her?"

"No. Oh, no ... no, you can't talk to her." Kate's voice dropped to a whisper. "She's dead, Shannon. Someone killed her."